gary soto

PETTY CRIMES

Harcourt, Inc.

ORLANDO AUSTIN NEW YORK SAN DIEGO TORONTO LONDON

www.HarcourtBooks.com

First Harcourt paperback edition 2006

The Library of Congress has cataloged the hardcover edition as follows:
Soto, Gary.
Petty crimes/Gary Soto.
p. cm.
Contents: La güera—Mother's clothes—Try to remember—The
boxing lesson—Your turn, Norma—The funeral suits—Little
scams—If the shoe fits—Frankie the rooster—Born worker.
Summary: A collection of short stories about Mexican American
youth growing up in California's Central Valley.
1. Mexican Americans—California—Juvenile fiction. 2. Children's
stories, American. [1. Mexican Americans—California—Fiction.
2. Short stories.] I. Title.
PZ7.S7242Pe 1998
[Fic]—dc21   97-37114
ISBN-13: 978-0-15-201658-6   ISBN-10: 0-15-201658-9
ISBN-13: 978-0-15-205437-3 pb   ISBN-10: 0-15-205437-5 pb

Text set in Perpetua
Designed by Lori McThomas Buley

C E G H F D B

Printed in the United States of America

For Susan Ferriss
and Ricardo Sandoval

TABLE OF CONTENTS

PETTY CRIMES

LA GÜERA

In kindergarten Priscilla and six other strawberry-cheeked girls and boys stood among Mexican and Hmong kids the color of earth. They all held hands, shared crayons and fingerpaints, and sang songs in what Priscilla thought was English but might have been Spanish. In any language, the songs were about a made-up world of rainbows, blue skies, and lakes as deep as her eyes. There were unicorns in these songs and *baa-baa*ing sheep as clean and fat as clouds.

Outside the school, the world was marked with graffiti, boom boxes, lean dogs behind fences, and gangsters with tattooed arms and chests. One old gangster, a *veterano* from way back, had a sombrero tattoo on his belly. When he laughed, the sombrero went up and down. Everywhere litter scuttled like rats in the streets, and the houses around the school were collapsing like mushrooms. There was no mercy in the anger that thrived in the bitter weeds.

Back then they called her Priscilla, but by sixth grade the other white kids had gone, taking with them the rainbows and the unicorns. She remained at Jefferson Elementary and took on another name. She was called La Güera because of her light skin. She was half white, half Mexican, but she felt like the Mexicans, or at least like the tough *cholas* whose eyes narrowed when a bomb—a car full of *vatos*—cruised past. Priscilla had become a homegirl. She teased her hair and darkened her lashes with mascara and spread a butterfly of greenish eye shadow over her lids.

La Güera and five of her friends huddled like sparrows in the oil-spotted parking lot in front of a 7-Eleven. Their breath was caught in the frosty morning. It puffed up and disappeared within seconds.

"Do it, girl," Dolores taunted, half meaning what she said about stealing from the store.

"They ain't going to catch you," Dolores continued. "I steal there all the time."

The girls wanted Chap Stick, and they wanted to curl their fingers around Mars bars and Butterfingers, a treasury of sweetness, something more than the sunflower seeds they cracked on their teeth and spit into the wind. They wanted excitement.

"They ain't going to do nothing," La Teri argued. She was Dolores's *carnala,* a tough *chola* who screamed when she got into fights and scratched other girls' faces until the skin built up under her fingernails. She seemed to have stopped growing, but to make up for her size, she fought hard. When she smiled, her fangs showed, white as milk.

"Get in there, girl!" Dolores commanded. "I do it all the time."

"Then you do it, *esa!*" La Güera snapped. "My mom's already mad at me." Earlier in the week, La Güera had rifled through her mom's purse and took Life Savers, chewing gum, and a small flashlight that she blinked against her palm at night. When her mom found out, she screamed that Priscilla was going to go to juvie, and then she would find out about life.

But suddenly La Güera, snapping gum that had lost all its sweetness, clicked her tongue and said, "I'll be back, *cholas.*"

She entered the 7-Eleven and immediately caught the eye of the guy behind the counter. He was ringing up a sale of miniature donuts, the boxed kind showing through a cellophane window. La Güera saw those donuts as herself, powdery white on the outside but brown at the core.

La Güera licked her lips and thought of only one thing—Chap Stick. She entered the aisle of medicines and scanned cough medicines, pain relievers, denture cleaners, dental floss—old-people stuff that she would never dream of buying. She knew she would never have to worry about those items. She would be dead before she got to that stage of life.

She had stolen before, usually from her mother; but sometimes at school, if a backpack was sitting alone against a wall, she would unzip the zipper and pull out sandwiches or a comb or a gnawed pencil. But this would be the first time she stole from a store. She picked up the cherry-flavored Chap Stick and hid it behind her palm like a cigarette. She walked toward the door, but the guy at the counter said, "Put it back!"

"*¡Qué!* What!" La Güera said, turning on her heels, a snarl on her lips.

"Whatever you got in your hands."

La Güera was nervous but not scared. Her fingernails were biting into her palm. She thought of her girls outside, and she thought of the man in front of her.

"White pig," La Güera yelled.

"You Mexicans think you can take what you want."

"White pig!" she repeated, unable to think of another insult. She hurled the Chap Stick at the man. She swung open the door and ran around the building, not looking back. Her friends were waiting.

"*El gavacho* almost snagged me!" La Güera said, out of breath.

The six girls ran.

But the taunt echoed in her head: "You Mexicans think you can take what you want." She liked that. She liked being Mexican, and muttered, "That white boy was nothing. I'll get Victor to mess him up if he calls the cops." Victor was a *vato loco* who could hurt someone with just a stare. He had gone to juvie five times, and fives times he'd gotten out and continued his routine of hostility and thievery. His knuckles were darkening with tattoos and scars, signs that he was not to be messed with.

The girls weren't upset that she had come back empty-handed because La Güera let loose with cuss words and threats that spooked even them. She pulled the girls to Safeway, where she said, "You wait outside." La Güera entered, zipping and un-zipping her windbreaker. When she returned ten minutes later, not in the least rushed, she opened her palm and revealed a Chap Stick. She told Dolores, "Feel in my pocket."

Dolores pushed her hand into La Güera's pocket and brought out candies, big ones, with wrappers that rustled like Christmas itself.

"White girl, you're *bad, muy mala,*" Dolores said. La Güera hugged her homegirl, and the others showed their respect by letting her walk in the middle. They took their candies and ate them at Holmes playground, where the dudes in cutoffs were shooting hoops or playing handball against the gym wall. The girls watched the boys and concluded, "They're worthless."

La Güera continued her rampage at stores, stealing candies, eyeliners, lipsticks, and Chap Stick until her face and lips were built up with sweetness and oils. Then her sweet tooth craved See's Candies, and she managed to lift boxes of toffee and cherry-filled chocolates as heavy as gold and almost as costly. She stole from Longs Drugs, carrying away a canister of imported Danish cookies sprinkled with diamond-bright sugar.

"You're bad, *esa*," the girls taunted, scared now of La Güera. She was on a binge that said she had problems, and the girls knew it.

Then they almost got caught at Mom-and-Pop Grocery. "Pop" was a burly man with a beard, like Santa. But unlike Santa, he wasn't giving things away. He chased after the girls, his belly slipping like a sack under his T-shirt. After that incident, the girls began to stay away from La Güera, even avoiding her in the hallways at school. *"Está loca,"* they said about her in the girls' bathroom, where they teased their hair and sucked on cigarettes.

"Yeah, what's wrong with the *chola*?" La Teri asked Dolores, who was puffing out her ratted hair with jabbing pokes of a pencil. She shrugged and responded, *"¿Quién sabe?"*

La Güera finally got caught stealing—not candies

but a whole cake she tried to lift from the display window at Blanco's Bakery. Her sweet tooth had grown. The police came this time, and she spent two days in juvie, where all her sweet tooth could plunge into was red or yellow Jell-O, the two kinds they served at dinner. The Jell-O kept her going, that and the raisins they served at lunch.

"What am I going to do with you, Priscilla?" La Güera's mother yelled as they drove home from juvie.

"I'm La Güera, not Priscilla," La Güera said.

"No, you're not!" her mother snapped. "And stop that Spanish. You sound like a *chola*!"

"*Pues, soy una chola,*" La Güera said in a near whisper. She didn't really listen to her mother plead for her to stop stealing. "It was *estúpido*," she told her mother. "I shouldn't have stole that cake."

Her mother's eyes were on the rearview mirror, as if the police were after them. She wiggled the steering wheel and said, "You better believe it was stupid!"

La Güera thought to herself, I should have taken the pig cookies instead of the cake.

La Güera went back to her old ways, but this time she went to another Mexican bakery. There, she stole the pig cookies. She was eating the feet off these cookies when the owner came running out and chased her, his white apron flying in the breeze of his fury.

She got away. And she got away with other robberies. She might have continued to get away, except for the morning her mother was vacuuming her room and found a horde of candies, mostly Kisses. Her mother ran her hands through the treasure of Kisses and, on her knees, with tears springing from her eyes, cried, "Why? Why is my daughter a thief?" She pulled the string of a Kiss and the aluminum foil uncurled, revealing a nipple of chocolate. She tossed the candy in her mouth.

Her mother sent La Güera away for a week. She would have sent her to an academy for delinquent girls, but those places were too expensive. So she sent her daughter to her sister, Carolyn, who lived in Stevens Point, Wisconsin.

"Be good, Priscilla," her mother cried at the airport.

"La Güera," La Güera corrected, the last words she said to her mother as she walked down the ramp to the waiting jet.

It was April, and the spring landscape in Wisconsin was like the landscape she had drawn in kindergarten: tulips pushing their bright heads through the earth and daffodils wagging like tongues in the breeze. The fields were ablaze with flowers. The trees were shaggy with blossoms, and bees greedily hopped from one plant to another. And, to La

Güera's surprise, the sky was actually as blue as a crayon.

Her aunt greeted her at the airport, calling, "My sweet Priscilla, it's so good to see you." La Güera corrected her aunt. "I'm La Güera, *tía*," she told her aunt as they walked toward the airport parking. She taught her aunt how to pronounce her name. Being a good sport, her aunt tried over and over. It came out "Laweera," and there it remained.

"*¿Qué son estos, tía?* What's that?" La Güera asked as she pointed a long, polished finger at some pigs gathered behind a fence. They were driving through the countryside toward the small farm where the family, still intact with husband and two daughters, lived.

"Why, those are hogs," her aunt said. "You've seen hogs before, haven't you?"

Hogs, La Güera thought. She had seen cows before, actually petted their noses, and once she'd fed a whole loaf of bread to two ducks in a lake. But hogs, she wasn't sure.

"We raise hogs, too," her aunt said. Her eyes were on the road, not the rearview mirror.

"You eat those animals?" La Güera asked.

Aunt Carolyn smiled. "Sometimes."

"They taste good," La Güera commented. She remembered that pork was the meat in *chile verde*, one of her favorite dishes.

9

They drove in silence, with the aunt looking every now and then at her niece. Finally she asked, "Priscilla?"

La Güera looked at her aunt, eyes narrowed.

"Laweera," her aunt said. "You're wearing make-up. It's maybe too much?"

La Güera had left Fresno with a scrubbed face, but in six hours of flights and connections, she had dolled herself up. Large butterfly-like strokes colored her eyes, and her lips were brown red. With an eyeliner, she had penciled in a blue tear.

"Es el estilo, tía," La Güera said.

Her two cousins were Brittany and Amber. Brittany was the oldest, at fifteen, and Amber was thirteen, but nearly as tall as her sister. La Güera was fourteen, so it was three girls born all in a row. Her two cousins were waiting in the driveway of a large house that looked like the house she had drawn in first grade when her eye-hand coordination was tops.

"Amber, Britt," their mother said, "meet your cousin." Her aunt hesitated, rolling her tongue in her mouth and getting ready to try her Spanish. Then she continued. "Meet your cousin, Laweera."

La Güera said, "Hey," and the girls returned her greeting with a long, drawn-out "Hellooooo." The two sisters were surprised that a girl their age was allowed to wear eyeliner, and lots of it.

"We're very happy that you'll be staying with us this week," Brittany said, smiling.

Uncle Bill approached them. Dressed in a plaid shirt, he was carrying a pail of nails. His hands were rough as wood, and his face was lined from working outdoors.

"You must be Priscilla," he said, smiling. He put down his pail and patted La Güera on the shoulder.

"That's right, Bill," said Aunt Carolyn. "But she goes by 'Laweera.' "

Bill nodded and smiled. He didn't even try to say her name.

The girls showed La Güera her bedroom, which held a canopy bed, frilly curtains, pictures of Little Bo-peep, and wallpaper as pink as her crayon in kindergarten. When she leaned out the window, La Güera saw a view of a pasture with sheep going *"baa baa."*

"They don't bite you?" La Güera asked of the sheep.

"No," Amber answered. Unable to stifle her curiosity, she asked, "How come you got your face like that?"

La Güera would have messed up the girl, but she figured that it was her cousin. She's stupid, she thought, but I better be nice.

"It's the way it is, homegirl," La Güera remarked. "That's how we do it in Califas."

The two girls took La Güera to the silo, and after that they showed her the barn, where a baby pig stood next to its mother.

"He was born last week," Amber said. Her freckles were like hay flecks, and her hair was the color of another crayon from childhood.

"You girls ever had *chile verde?*" asked La Güera.

"What's that?" Brittany asked.

"Mexican food. The best," La Güera answered.

The girls shrugged and patted the little pig's stomach.

They rode the tractor back and forth that afternoon, and La Güera laughed when they dipped over a small bump in the muddy field. "I'm hitting the switch," she said, thinking about the hydraulics on a lowrider. La Güera chewed on three Milky Ways as she rode the tractor. She had found them in a jar in the kitchen, and she figured that she was a guest and she was hungry, so she helped herself.

The next day they went fishing, which La Güera thought would be boring. And it was. The fishing pole hung over the rush of a river, and the fish— trout, they promised—stayed away, shimmering across the water, where the girls could see their tails flop occasionally. But during that time, La Güera made up Brittany's face, using the hundred-plus lipsticks, eyeliners, and blushes she kept in a purse, stuff that was all stolen.

"You look good, girl," La Güera chimed. She

painted her cousin with mascara and eye shadow, and teased her hair so it rose up like a whip.

Brittany stood up and bent her face over the water.

"What do you think?" La Güera asked.

The water rippled from mosquitoes and insects and the push of the current.

"I look...really different," Brittany said, brushing back the whip of hair that had fallen over her eyes. "It's like Halloween."

Amber said she didn't like it and she would never, never wear makeup. "I'm not *ever* going to Fresno," she said angrily.

"Be quiet," Brittany told her younger sister.

La Güera felt like beating up Amber, but she was her cousin. So she just clicked her tongue and said, "Get with it, girl."

Then Brittany worked on La Güera, adding more this and more that, and by the time they returned to the farm, La Güera had given Brittany a street name, La Peaches, because she was soft as that fruit and almost as golden.

"I'm never going to Fresno if I have to look like that," Amber pouted. She threw herself on her bed and read through *Seventeen*, noticing that the models used makeup, but not that much.

But by the end of the week's vacation, Amber was caked up with makeup and her name was La Luz, for she gave off a summery light.

The girls became a gang, Las Farm Girls, which they knew was a joke as temporary as La Güera's stay. They walked around downtown Stevens Point, where three men, one as large as Humpty-Dumpty, came out from a sporting goods store and whistled at them. In Spanish, with her hands stiffened into a gang sign that meant "I'll be back, homes," La Güera told them to shut up or she was going to scratch their faces. Brittany and Amber were breathless from fear.

But they hung with their cousin. They didn't think much of taking the tractor from the field to the road. They stole from a store, and sold one of their pups without telling their parents. Aunt Carolyn had had enough. She made them scrub their faces until their skin hurt and handed them the fishing poles.

"Go try again!" La Güera's aunt said, with her husband at her side, a silent man who worked the fields and didn't say much. "And no more nonsense, Priscilla!"

La Güera didn't bother to correct her. She took a pole and rattled a box of peanut brittle she found on top of the refrigerator.

After a week she went away with more than she had come with. She had most of her aunt Carolyn's makeup, plus a stinky perfume she would have thrown from the jet if the windows had opened.

———

La Güera continued stealing, but not candies and makeup. She stole La Teri's boyfriend, Ruben, a guy lanky as a giraffe. He was average in looks, but La Güera wanted more than a pretty face and candy. She needed some hugs, big arms to wrap her in warmth.

"You better leave my dude alone," La Teri threatened at school while she and La Güera cleaned the gym wall slashed with graffiti, which included their names. "I'll scratch your eyes out!"

"Wake up, girl! He don't like you," La Güera said, swallowing the last pill of an M&M. "He says you don't kiss good."

That's when they began fighting. La Teri slapped La Güera with a paintbrush, and everyone stepped back, even a security guard, who was eating a bologna sandwich. They gave the girls room for the inevitable.

"You ain't nothing," La Teri screamed. Like a cat, her claws had come out.

"He says you smell, *flaca,*" La Güera snarled. With a dripping brush, she smacked La Teri, and a white splotch covered the side of *her* head.

"My man loves me," La Teri cried, and struck again with the brush.

"He says you don't kiss good," La Güera repeated, hurting from the blow.

"You lie!"

They smacked each other with the paintbrushes again and then threw down their brushes. La Teri pulled La Güera's hair, and La Güera ground a fist into La Teri's ear.

"He loves me," La Teri sobbed.

"You kiss like a grandma," La Güera said through her own tears, which had ruined her makeup.

La Teri threw a punch that knocked La Güera back on her heels. La Teri shook her former *carnala,* shook her until everything spilled from that girl: candies, eyeliner, eyebrow pencils, nail polish, and lipsticks—the years when the sky was as blue as crayon. She shook La Güera, ripped her with her fingernails. La Güera's blood was a crayon color, her hair was crayon, her biting teeth were crayon.

"He loves me!" La Teri cried.

"You don't kiss good," La Güera moaned.

The girls struggled, hand to hand, like dancers, their faces pressed over each other's shoulders. They groaned and cussed. Now, in seventh grade, their world looked hard and gray, like cement. The crayon-blue sky was gone forever.

MOTHER'S CLOTHES

Cancer wasn't an arm as thin as straw, yellowish skin, dented cheeks, or a leg limp as a garden hose in the sun. Cancer wasn't a crab inside the body, eating at liver and spleen, or kidneys the color of eggplant. Cancer wasn't the C word whispered in front of La Virgen de Guadalupe or the short, stubby candle lit in the monstrous shadows of Saint Alphonso. Cancer wasn't what occurred across town. It was here.

It was here in Alma's mother like a frog that bloated up her stomach. When Alma hugged her mother every night before bed, she felt the liquids of the disease that would drain only in death. And her mother's death was slow—four long seasons until, finally, in spring, when the blossoms were blown into the air like confetti, Alma's mother died. She was buried under the blossoms.

"It was so beautiful," Alma would say later.

And it was. Blossoms scented the world. It had rained a day earlier, and the sky was blue as an eye. A reef of clouds passed, pulling with it rain and thunder.

Alma was fourteen, tall like her father, but watchful like her mother, always picking up clues and rumors, innuendos. She knew that her mother and father hadn't been getting along. They had thrown fierce looks at each other. They had slammed screen doors, revved engines, walked on stiletto heels of anger. But once cancer had shown up on the X rays, their anger disappeared like smoke, and for the first time Alma could remember, they became kind to each other.

After the funeral her father sent Alma away for a week. She stayed in Los Angeles with her aunt, who cried over cups of coffee, saying that her sister—Alma's mother, all of thirty-four—was too young to be taken into the arms of our Lord. She showed Alma photo albums of the sisters when they were young. Alma's mother's smile was natural, her hair piled with looping curls, her legs stork-thin in a miniskirt. Her aunt even showed Alma a scar her mother had left behind.

"Here," her aunt said, offering her forearm. "She threw a toy truck at me. Feel it."

Alma felt the velvety slickness of the scar. My mother did this, she thought, almost with pride.

When she returned from Los Angeles, Alma noticed that the house was clean. Where her mother had sat on the couch, huge with disease, there was a new slipcover. The old magazines were gone, the bills from the doctors had been taken away, perhaps paid, perhaps tossed in the garbage. The face of the TV had been wiped clean of dust and static. The curtains had been taken down and cleaned. The carpet had been shampooed. Her father had even changed the bulbs in the lamps.

"You really cleaned up the house, Dad," Alma told her father, who had ordered a pizza for Alma's return. Together they sat in front of the TV.

"Yeah, it looks pretty nice," her father said, glancing at her a second, then turning his face back to the TV. The San Francisco Giants were playing. The score could have been a hundred to one for all Alma cared. She counted the sausages on each slice of pizza—an average of three, half covered with cheese. She noticed that her father had a beer on the TV tray, something that he had given up while her mother was ill.

"Come on," her father shouted to the television, to a player on the field of light. "*¡Ay, Dios!* I can't believe they're paid this much to mess up an easy grounder."

"*Papi,* are we going to move?" Alma asked. The pizza, shaped like a wagging tongue, weighed in her hands. She thought that her father had cleaned up the house to sell it.

Her father looked at his daughter.

"Of course not! We should get new furniture," he said. He pounded his recliner and added, "In fact, I'm going to toss this beast."

And he did, and much more. Piece by piece, he got rid of the old furniture—recliner, gutless couch, and a coffee table as wobbly as a table in a restaurant. He got rid of the dusty, gilt-framed print of a frowning clown clutching straw flowers. Vases went, and so did lamps, mirrors, clocks that were always minutes behind. Even their aged cat, Lucky, went away, although her father claimed that he hadn't taken the cat to the pound.

"He was old," her father said. "He probably went away..." He stopped, but Alma filled in the last words, "...to die."

Except for losing Lucky, Alma didn't mind the changes. Her father chucked things like a madman. He began to air out the house on cold days, and he gave things to the Salvation Army: pots and pans, electric blankets, irons, bundles of bedsheets and towels. She didn't mind until one day she discovered that he had given away all her mother's clothes, every stitch—dresses, pants, jackets and sweaters, hats and vests, shoes and sandals. Even her aprons.

"How could you!" she screamed at her father.

His eyes became watery, distant. He sat down in

his new recliner, his limp arms folded across his lap.

"Mom's been dead only two months," she cried from the new couch, bright with printed flowers.

"*Mi'ja*, we have to start over," her dad said, his arms flying up as he begged for her to understand.

That was his answer. That was his answer to everything. He argued that life was bitter as a penny. He begged her to understand that he was doing his best.

Alma might have forgotten about the clothes, except a week later, while she was at the 7-Eleven, she saw a woman wearing her mother's blue sweater. For a moment Alma thought it *was* her mother. The woman was the same height, and her hair was curled.

"Oh no!" she caught herself saying.

The woman stood in front of the dry cleaner's and appeared to be waiting for someone. She was looking off in the distance, across the street. Alma followed the woman's gaze and saw children coming home in groups of threes and fours. Then the woman suddenly smiled at her, a smile that was easy and natural. Alma turned away and saw her face reflected in the window of the 7-Eleven. It held an expression of horror.

Since they lived in a small town with more second-hand stores than fashionable boutiques, with dozens of Saturday-morning yard sales and a grand swap meet at the drive-in, Alma imagined that her mother's clothes were being worn everywhere in the town. She imagined women zipping into dresses, buttoning blouses, tugging legs into pants, smoothing their sweaters of wrinkles before they left the house. She imagined these women before mirrors, turning in the silvery light. She saw them shrugging into her mother's jackets, her shoes. And she imagined the socks tumbling in dryers, or weeping gray tears from the clotheslines. Her mother's bras cupped other flesh, and her hats shielded another pair of eyes in rain and sun. The clothes were scattered about town, and Alma vowed to get them back.

A few days later in front of the school, as parents were dropping off children, Alma saw the mother of one of her classmates. The woman was wearing her mother's green coat, the one that her father had bought her for their tenth anniversary. Alma remembered that coat. Her mother had worn it the year she took Alma to sit in Santa's lap at Kmart.

"Mom," Alma caught herself saying to this woman.

The car lurched and disappeared, but not before the woman glanced at Alma and smiled. Alma moved her mouth, thinking, Am I smiling?

Her schoolmate was Helena Sanchez, a quiet girl like Alma. They had two classes together, Biology and English. It was during English that Alma whispered, "I have to talk to you."

Helena didn't understand. She pointed a finger at herself and mouthed, "Me?"

Alma simply nodded her head. She snapped shut the rings of her binder with a hard click.

During break Alma pulled Helena to a bench, and there the two sat in silence. Alma's eyes cut upward to a plane crossing the cloudless sky. It might land, she thought, or it might crash. Then there would be more dead people.

"What did you want, Alma?" Helena asked. It was, after all, recess, their fifteen minutes to mingle and talk. Silence would not do.

Alma gripped the bench, and she said, "My mother died."

"I know," Helena said almost callously. She corrected it with sympathy. "I'm sorry that she died."

Alma bit her lower lip.

"Your mother's wearing my mom's coat."

Helena picked up her backpack, hugging it like a teddy bear.

"No, she's not," Helena responded.

Alma said again that she was and described how her mother had worn it when she took Alma to see Santa. She said that if Helena examined the left sleeve she'd see a dark spot.

"It's nail polish," Alma explained. "She got some on it. I remember. She was doing her nails—"

"You're lying," Helena interrupted.

Alma shook her head.

"Why are you doing this?" Helena whispered into the collar of Alma's coat, they were so close. She looked over Alma's shoulder at her other classmates. "I said I was sorry that your mother is dead."

"I want my mother's clothes back," Alma said.

"I'm telling you my mom doesn't have your mother's coat."

"She does! She bought it from a secondhand store."

Helena got up and stomped away, shrugging the weight of her backpack angrily onto her shoulders.

Alma cried. After school she waited for Helena's mother to pull up to the curb for her daughter. When she saw their car approach, Alma's heart thumped. She was working up the nerve to ask for the coat. With six dollars in her purse, she was going to buy it back.

The car pulled to the curb, crunching the backs of leaves herded by wind into the gutter. Alma ran to the car and peered through the window, freckled with raindrops from an earlier shower. She knocked on the window, and the mother, startled, touched her chest. Then her face softened.

"What is it?" she asked, the electric windows lowering.

Helena's mother wasn't wearing the green coat. Instead, she had on a brown trench coat, the belt pulled tightly. Her waist was as thin as a wasp's.

"Nothing," Alma said. She stepped away from the window. She turned and saw Helena approaching, her shoulders hunched, the backpack like the hump of a camel.

"It's not your mother's coat!" Helena argued. "I told you already!"

Alma turned away, pushing through the crowds of students waiting for parents and relatives. She didn't want to confront either Helena or her mother.

Alma stayed away from Helena during that week at school. On the weekend she decided to search secondhand stores. She stopped first at the Goodwill store on Maple Avenue and then at the less popular Saint Vincent de Paul down the street. Alma didn't find her mother's clothes in either place. She did see her dad's old recliner at Goodwill. She sat in it, tilting the seat back like a dentist's chair. She sighed the way her father might sigh after a long day on his feet at the post office where he worked. She also spotted a lamp and the wobbly coffee table, a film of dust aging them even more.

"Don't play on the furniture," a man called from across the store.

"It used to be ours!" Alma responded, sitting up. "We gave it to you."

The man seemed to be thinking hard about what he had heard. His forehead reflected a square of light. His mouth was a gash. The gash moved and said, "Still, don't play."

Alma patted the recliner, that old dog of furniture, and left.

But at the Salvation Army she found her mother's white Liz Claiborne sweater. She held the sweater against her own body, which was much thinner than her mother's.

"It's Mom's," Alma whispered. She sniffed the sleeves, pulling in the scent of her mother, the last remnant of her body on this earth. Alma draped the sweater across her arm and continued exploring.

She found eight pairs of shoes, a pair of blue jeans, worn white at the knees, and plenty of her mother's pants hanging on racks. She found five blouses together, as they might have been arranged in her mother's closet. She searched the racks and piles of clothes, some musty and sour, others washed. She looked around the store and saw that there were other girls her age, pulling at the clothes in the racks, sifting.

Are their mothers dead, too? she wondered.

The girls searched frantically.

They must be, Alma thought. She watched the angelic face of a girl who might have been eighteen. Her face seemed white from loneliness, bloodless.

Alma felt sorry for the other girls.

"They have no mothers," she said to herself, the crook of her arm now heavy with clothes.

Alma returned to her own business. She found three belts, their buckles clanging like chimes. She found slippers and hats, a scarf that was blood-red. She ran it through her fingers. She found all her mother's purses tangled in a bin. She fumbled through each purse and located bobby pins and a barrette. She found an evening gown with a bib of lace. She found more tops and blouses, almost a whole wardrobe—everything that could help to assemble a memory.

Alma knew that she had only eight dollars and some change. Still, she went up to the cashier, her arms weighted with clothes, and heaved everything onto the counter.

"Here," she told the woman, whose eyes were bluish with eye shadow. "These were my mom's."

"Come again?" the woman asked, her hand reaching for a pencil poked into her tall, bushlike hair. Her bifocals hung around her neck.

"Mom is dead," she said. "She died of cancer, and my dad gave all her clothes away."

The woman slipped on her bifocals, something she needed for such a moment.

"Your dad gave them away?" she asked, studying Alma, then the clothes piled on the counter.

Alma wasn't timid. Her mother was dead, buried under the eternal heaviness of grass and packed earth. What could scare Alma now? If she had to, she would run from the store with these clothes. She told the woman that she wanted to get her mother's clothes back.

"Young lady," the woman said, her bifocals slipping down. "Young lady, let me get some plastic bags."

Alma got her mother's clothes back and borrowed a shopping cart. The wheels of the cart clacked over cracks on the way home. In her bedroom she locked the door and began to assemble outfits. She put the white sweater together with the blue pants. She put the beige pants with the khaki top. The pleated trousers went with the embroidered white shirt. She matched outfits and worked out new combinations. In her mind, she could see her mother reaching for the green pumps, the white flats, her sandals, dark from wear. She could almost see her mother, as she had known her before the cancer. Alma placed the red scarf against the sweater and said, "It's nice."

A knock sounded at the front door. Her dad was at the gym, the house quietly creaking from a storm. When the knock sounded again, Alma hurried from her bedroom to see who it was. She pulled back the curtain to discover Helena standing there.

Alma opened the door.

"My mom said to give it back," Helena said, searching Alma's face. She held out the green coat. "She said . . . ," Helena started, then stopped.

"Come in," Alma said.

Helena hesitated, her front teeth like claws pulling at her lower lip.

"OK," she said. "Just for a little while. My mom said that she's really sorry about your mother."

"Thanks. It's OK."

Alma took the coat from Helena and led her friend by the hand to her bedroom.

"See what I'm doing," Alma said brightly. "I got all her clothes back—or most of them, I think."

The room was musty.

Alma pushed away the outfit she had assembled. She laid her mom's green coat on the bed.

"Let's start over," Alma suggested, scrambling the outfit on the bed. "What do you think would go with the coat?"

"Huh?"

Alma explained again how she was putting together outfits.

"Like Barbie's clothes—remember?" she asked.

"I think I better go," Helena said. She turned, her gaze falling on the doorknob.

"No! No!" Alma pleaded. She touched Helena's arm, then slid her hand down to Helena's, which she squeezed like a sponge. "Please, Helena—stay."

"OK. Just a little while."

Helena considered the clothes, her gaze raking over the piles draped on chairs, table, bedposts in wonderment. She looked down at the shoes, all parked in a line like cars.

"I don't know," Helena muttered.

"OK, I'll start," Alma said. "Pretend it's spring and she needs to go see a friend in the hospital."

Alma placed a pair of black slacks on the bed, smoothing out the wrinkles.

"Ah," Helena said. "She should wear that top."

Helena pointed to the purple silk long-sleeved blouse, the one she had worn when the doctor diagnosed her cancer.

Alma hesitated. "Yeah, but maybe she should wear the red sleeveless." Her finger went up to her mouth. "You see, it's spring, but it's really hot for that time of year."

"Oh," Helena muttered.

"Yeah, it's really hot," Alma said.

"That's right," Helena said, playing along now. "It's really hot, so she's wearing the sleeveless."

Outside, rain beat on the windows. Wind picked up and howled past the glass.

"It's summer now," Alma said.

Rain thumped and flowed through the gutters. Rain gathered in pools near the drain. Rain flowed like rivers in the leaf-choked gutters.

The girls moved through the seasons—spring, summer, fall, and, finally, winter, when the days were short and the sun no more than a smudge of light almost breaking through the valley fog. They started over, bringing in the green coat.

"See the nail polish?" Alma said.

Helena nodded.

They assembled wool pants and tucked a heavy cotton shirt inside the green coat. They fixed the collars of both the shirt and the coat.

"We need gloves," Helena said, glancing about, really getting into this game.

Alma found a pair of gloves, crumpled like letters. They were white and out of season, but she placed them at the cuffs of the coat, where her mother's hands would have been had she been alive, had she been preparing for the day.

"There," Alma said, stepping back. "She is ready to go."

TRY TO REMEMBER

Laura sat in her grandparents' living room, sat with her fingers angled into a steeple. She yawned, her mouth shaped like the O of a choir girl, and tears washed over her eyes. She was sleepy from the overheated living room. Steam gathered and wept from the front window. Plants drooped. Sneakers, a tiny Chihuahua, panted on his mat. Dust particles floated like stars and planets. Laura waved her hand through this galaxy of dust, rearranging its order. It was something to do that long Sunday. She was bored in her grandparents' house, sitting on the couch and waiting and waiting for the time when she could go home.

The living room was red as a Valentine's Day card, and Laura attributed the bold colors to the fact that her grandparents were from Mexico, where life itself was more vibrant, like tropical flowers or birds with long, clacking beaks. The couch and love seat were red velour, and even the wall-to-wall carpet was red. The lamp shades were the tint of fiery chiles. A Bible, large as a telephone book, was wrapped in white chiffon.

Laura thought—and she hated herself for thinking it—that her grandparents had no taste. Of course, she would never have said so, especially on a Sunday. Still, it troubled her when her grandmother Catalina wore the bandanna on her head that said: GAY PAREE! OOO-LA-LA.

Outside, the gray fog pressed its shoulders to the front window while Laura sat on the couch, her *Seventeen* already devoured from cover to glossy cover. Along with Grandmother, her parents had gone to look at a used car they'd spotted in the newspaper. She had nothing to do, except to watch a Mexican game show, *Siempre en Domingo,* on television. Like her grandparents' living room, the game show was loud. The music blared, and Laura thought the game-show host could have been a used-car salesman, oily as his receding hair.

Her grandfather, who had been sleeping, suddenly awoke, kicking off one slipper. His eyes blinked. He moaned and stretched, and reached for the slipper, which he fit back onto his foot. He pressed his palm to his whiskery mouth, adjusting his dentures.

"Did you sleep good?" Laura asked.

Her grandfather ignored her question.

"*Mi'ja,*" Grandfather Benito said, "I didn't pass my test. I can't drive no more."

Her grandfather had gone to his auto insurance company, where he had taken a test. He was seventy, the age when his insurance company became cautious of older drivers.

"They gave me a list of words," he continued, this time in Spanish. "I got four right." He waited for his granddaughter to respond.

Laura asked in English, "What do you mean, Grandpa?"

He explained that the insurance agent had given him a list of ten words, and he was allowed to memorize the list for five minutes. Then he had to recall at least seven of the words.

"I only got four," he lamented. He recalled how his mind had gone blank as paper after recalling the four words he did get right. He shook his head like a horse. "The words I got were *mirror, squirrel, possibly,* and *light switch.*"

"They gave you a test?" she asked. "You're not in school, or anything. Can they do that?"

Grandfather Benny gripped his recliner. A wild eye turned on Laura.

"*¡Mantequilla!*" he yelled. He turned his large head toward her. "It was *butter.* That was one of the words."

His chest heaved, as if he were out of breath from

struggling to put on a T-shirt that was too small. But his excitement slowly subsided. He leaned back, eyes now dim, his work-worn hands resting on the arms of the recliner.

"Are you sick, Grandpa?" Laura asked after a moment. She had heard of Alzheimer's, but that illness had nothing to do with her. Until now, she thought. She scooted over on the couch, so that she faced her grandfather.

"How could I forget *butter*?" he asked. And it *was* odd. He loved butter on his tortillas, a little pat on his *frijoles*, butter on his steaming corn. He even used butter for burns and rashes.

"I forget things all the time," Laura said, a statement that was untrue but that she hoped would comfort her grandfather. In truth, her mind, like a sponge, sucked up everything—schoolwork, the names of rocks, gossip. Especially gossip.

Grandfather Benny pushed himself up from the recliner and shuffled into a kitchen painted as yellow as a banana. Laura followed, along with Sneakers, his stiff tail wagging. She thought her grandfather was going to pull out the butter from the refrigerator to make some point about his memory. Instead, he peeled a business card held by a magnet from the face of the refrigerator. It read, Rios Auto and Home Insurance.

"I just need two more," he said. He thumbed the business card. "Just two more words, *mi'ja*."

Laura watched her grandfather as he squinted, the furrows of his brow working the juices of his mind. She was worried for him.

"You help me," he said.

"How?"

He fumbled for a pencil and a piece of paper in a drawer, and, prodding Laura, went into the dining room. Laura sat where her grandfather usually sat, and it felt awkward, like sitting in a bathtub with no water.

"Give me a test," her grandfather said. "Write out five words."

"Five words," she repeated in a near whisper. Her gaze had already started to float around the dining room in search of those five words.

"But make them easy," he continued. "*Pues*, English is so difficult, *mi'ja*."

They sat at the table, and Laura clacked the pencil between her teeth. Using her free hand as a shield, she printed out carefully *clock, sugar bowl, eraser, statue*, and *remember*. Then, stern as a teacher, she snapped a look at her grandfather.

"Are you ready?" she asked.

He nodded.

She gave him the list, and his lips dryly mumbled each of the words. But he became confused when he glanced at *remember*.

"How come you got that one?" he asked. His index finger tapped the paper.

Laura glanced at the paper.

"It's just a word," she said. "Just like the other ones."

The refrigerator clicked on with a hum. Sneakers clicked around the kitchen. Her grandfather munched the tips of his wild mustache.

"OK," he said, holding the piece of paper like a menu. His eyes hardened like marbles as he began to memorize the words while Laura kicked her legs and kept time from the clock on the wall. She allowed her grandfather one minute extra. After all, he was her grandpa.

"Time!" Laura shouted, grasping for the list from his hands. "OK, tell me."

Grandpa sat up straight, eyed the clock, and then slowly let his shoulders slouch.

"*Pues,* there's *clock,* then *sugar*...and what's that thing called that goes like this?"

His hands wiggled in the air.

Laura hesitated, but then said, "Grandpa, I can't tell you."

"But I would know it in Spanish," he scolded.

Laura couldn't help herself.

"What is it then? In Spanish."

His face froze.

"I don't remember," he whispered, and raised his face toward the clock, which read 2:34. Then, in a soft voice, he countered: "When I was a boy, we didn't have that thing on top of the pencil."

"Try to remember."

Grandfather touched his nose with his finger. He rolled a pinch of his eyebrows between his thumb and index finger.

"Eraser," Laura said.

"Eso es," he said, pointing at Laura, his face as bright as a pumpkin. "OK, I got *sugar, eraser,* and . . . What was the other one?"

Laura sucked in her lips, not wanting to say anything.

"Ay, I got it already!" he whined. "You can tell me."

Laura didn't like this mental exercise. Her skinny legs no longer kicked but hung like rope. She wished her grandfather hadn't made her give him a test.

"It was *clock.*"

He smiled.

"That's it, so I got two more to go."

His sigh moved the plastic rose set in the middle of the table.

"The other words," he mumbled, "the other words are . . ."

Laura wanted to get up from the table and return to the living room, where the television hollered commercial jingles. She had known her grandfather as a hardworking man, one who guided wheelbarrows of cement all his life, who raised eight children, who played softball for Treviño's Restaurant until he was in his fifties. What was happening now?

"In Spanish, the word is *estatua,*" Laura said, willing to give him any hint that would get her away from the table. "It's almost like English."

"*Ay, statue,*" he shouted. "How could I forget?"

He should have known the word. Laura had made him a statue of a bird when she was in fourth grade. It still sat, one wing broken off, in his garden and was sprayed daily when Grandpa Benny took a hose to everything.

Now her grandfather felt confident. "Just one more," he said. He scratched his ear, which was a nest of wiry hair, and then pulled on an earlobe. He drummed his fingers on the table. He sighed and winced.

"It's like your favorite song, 'Tu Recuerdo y Yo,' " Laura said. "But in English."

"*Pues,* of course—*you!*"

Laura shook her head.

"Oh, I mean *recuerdo!*"

"But in English, Grandpa."

"It's *remember,*" he yelled. "That was easy."

Laura told her grandfather that he did good.

"You should take the insurance test again," she suggested.

"No, I'm just getting old, *mi'ja,*" he said sadly. He rose stiffly from his chair and started to the living room. He thanked his granddaughter and said that she should come up with five more words.

"I need to practice," he informed her. "For myself, not Mr. Rios."

Laura wished she was at home.

"Just give me a few minutes to rest," he said, walking toward the living room.

Laura went into the kitchen, where she poured milk into a saucepan and set it on a burner. Even though the house was stuffy, she wanted hot chocolate. While the milk was heating, she looked out the kitchen window—the valley fog hovered in the yard, nearly eclipsing the porch light. She shaded her brow and tried to make out the statue of her bird. But it was lost in the fog and the approaching evening.

Laura shivered, pressed against the icy window, and when she heard the milk hiss like a snake, she turned on her heels and hurried to the stove. She didn't want to singe the pan, which would make it difficult to wash.

While pouring the milk into a cup, her wrist grazed against the pan.

"*¡Ay!*" Laura screamed, and then let the pan of milk slip from her hand. The hot milk leaped up when it hit the floor and licked her leg.

Grandfather yelled from the living room, "*¿Qué pasó?* What are you doing?"

She could hear his shuffling steps as he raised the hem of her dress and looked at the burn, which was pink as a slap. She tried blowing on it, but her breath couldn't reach the burn.

"How come the milk is on the floor?" he asked.

"I burned myself," Laura whimpered.

Grandfather bent down and, taking her knee into his hands, examined the scald. Without saying anything, he rose with a groan and stepped over to the refrigerator. He began to shove bottles, plastic containers, foil-covered leftovers, and packages aside.

"There's no butter," he said, confused.

"I'll be OK," Laura said. But she admitted to herself that the scald hurt. And her wrist didn't feel much better, either. She reached for the towel hanging on the handle of the stove. She let it fall to the floor and, with her shoe, positioned the towel, which absorbed the spilled milk.

"What you need is butter," her grandfather said. "Or it'll become a scar."

"But I'm OK," Laura said. She examined her knees and compared the two: one was brown and the other pink as candy.

"No, we need butter," he argued.

Grandfather left the kitchen, and Laura continued sopping up the spilled milk. She picked up the dish towel, held it above the sink, and wrung it out. The towel wept milky tears.

"*¿Estás lista?*" her grandfather asked, zipping up his jacket.

"Ready for what?" she asked.

"To go to the store. For butter."

Laura's eyes grew large as olives.

"It's OK. It hardly hurts at all."

But her grandfather wouldn't hear of it. He prodded her to the living room, where she slipped into a sweater.

"But, Grandpa," she whined on the front porch. She wanted to remind him that the insurance company didn't allow him to drive. But she couldn't hurt his feelings.

"Don't you think we should leave a note?" she asked.

"*¡Ven!*" he yelled.

Laura climbed into the car, which was cold. She puffed out a plume of breath and watched it float and tear apart.

Grandfather got in and turned the key. He revved the engine, then felt for his wallet, a habit when he left the house. As he slowly backed the car out of the driveway, Laura fumbled for her seat belt, which she secured with a click.

"Your headlights, Grandpa," she warned.

"I can see!" he said roughly. Still, he turned them on when the car swung out onto the asphalt. He drove down the street, the fall leaves scattering about.

"You did good on your test," Laura lied. She wanted to encourage her grandfather, especially as they turned onto Hazel Street and gradually accelerated toward Tulare Street. She had a feeling that Grandpa Benny might at any moment forget how to drive and run the car into a storefront or jump a divider and run straight into a truck. He might just forget which pedal was for gas and which one was for braking. There was no telling what might happen on this strange evening.

Grandfather didn't say anything. He leaned over the steering wheel, jiggling it.

"You did real good," Laura repeated. She told him that he would probably pass the next time around.

"*¿Cómo?*" he asked.

Not only was his memory failing, Laura thought to herself, but his hearing, too.

"Nothing," she shouted. "*Nada.*"

The ancient Chevy swung onto Tulare Street, and it was then that Laura saw her dad's car. It passed quickly, but not before Laura's grandmother locked her eyes on her granddaughter's.

"It's Dad's car," Laura yelled. She got on her good knee, turned, and looked back. Her grandmother had also turned and stared at Laura. Then, slowly, her dad's car disappeared into the bank of fog.

"It was Dad's car," Laura repeated. She felt as if she had been kidnapped, and for a brief moment thought of leaping from the car when it stopped at a signal. But the urge passed.

"You drive good," Laura said to her grandfather.

"How come you're saying that?" he asked.

Craning her neck, Laura peered out the windshield. She imagined for a fraction of a second that her grandfather was driving in the wrong lane. But the car seemed steady.

"Oh, because...," Laura answered. "I don't know."

Her grandfather pulled into a 7-Eleven, but not before the Chevy stalled in the middle of the street and he pounded the steering wheel and called the car names.

As they parked at the 7-Eleven, Laura announced her plan. She had arrived at it when the car had stalled.

"Grandpa, I'm going to walk home," she said. "You get the butter and let me see if I can beat you home." She smiled a huge toothy smile shiny as scissors.

"*¿Cómo?*" he asked, confused. "You're talking *loca*."

"It's a...test for me," Laura countered.

"You're going to walk home?"

Laura nodded.

Her grandfather made a face and got out of the car. She saw him limp toward the door and saw that he was padding about in slippers. On a closer look, she noticed that one of the slippers was her grandmother's. She slowly pushed open the door, the icy air swirling about her face. She got out.

"Poor Grandpa," she said to no one. She watched her grandfather walk down the aisle of refrigerated foods. He opened one door after another. She wondered if he knew what he was getting there—butter, milk, soda, or beer? Who knows, she thought, he might buy firewood even though his house has no chimney.

"Try to remember," she coached quietly. "It's butter. You can do it."

But Grandfather kept opening the doors, searching.

Laura sidled away from the car. She crossed Tulare Street and stood in the middle of the divider. She looked back at the 7-Eleven and could see that her grandfather was at the checkout counter.

"Poor Grandpa," she said again. She saw that he was buying milk and perhaps butter. There was a small item in his hand.

She turned and, her skirt jumping above her scalded knee, ran across the street. Evening had lowered its weight all over the neighborhood. She ran and stopped, breathing hard.

"It's only four blocks to home," she said to herself. She didn't feel proud leaving her grandfather there. Still, she thought it was safer to walk home.

She walked in the thickening fog and wondered if it was like the climate her grandfather lived in, now that he was seventy and forgetting everything, including his favorite, butter.

THE BOXING LESSON

One hot, slow day, Rudy Herrera rummaged through his *abuelito*'s garage, fumbling through boxes and drawers and stepping over an ancient push mower, barbells, and battered furniture. He was checking things out because he was bored, and his mom and his grandfather were in the kitchen talking *chisme*. They'll be crowing for hours, he figured.

In one drawer, he found a tape recorder that was shaped like a Zippo lighter. It was solid chrome, heavy, something made long ago, maybe during World War II, maybe earlier, maybe even before his grandfather was born. He turned the miniature tape recorder over, examining it, and opened up the back. The tape was tiny and the battery was as small as a button on a cuff.

"This is bad," he told his grandfather when he carried it inside.

His *abuelito* said that it belonged to Chuy Sanchez, a guy he had known in the service during the Korean War.

"He was a spy," his grandfather whispered, not wanting to be heard.

"You're playing with me," Rudy said, but hoping it was true that he was holding in his thirteen-year-old hands the tools of a spy.

"*No, muchacho,*" his grandfather said. He told a story about how Chuy had been asked by none other than Dwight D. Eisenhower to put on a North Korean uniform, cut across the demilitarized zone, and check things out.

"They never heard from him again," his grandfather said, clouds of memory roaming across his eyes.

"*¡Híjole!* He got caught." Rudy whistled, moved by the story. Rudy imagined that the North Koreans must have pushed bamboo up his fingernails, kungfued him for the fun of it, and called him all sorts of names Chuy couldn't understand. But he also pictured him as a solid type, someone who wouldn't squeal.

His grandfather gave him the tape recorder.

"You're spoiling the boy," Rudy's mother said. Donut crumbs floated in her coffee.

Abuelito chuckled, his belly moving up and down on his lap. In return, he asked Rudy to cut his lawn.

———

Rudy was clever. He got the tape recorder to work, and during the long days of summer, he recorded sounds—birds, car screechings, clothes in the dryer, his mother humming over her potted geraniums, and even a *pedo* his father threw up in the air.

"That's not me," his father laughed when his son played it back while they stood on the porch.

"That's your *pedo,*" Rudy said.

"No, mine's like this."

His father lit one that woke their cat, Menso, who blinked and looked around, its whiskers twitching.

Rudy laughed and went on recording. He recorded everything—a screen door slamming, the sprinkler hurling water, *refritos* hissing in a black iron pan—and then he got serious. He recorded his private thoughts, like how he liked a girl named Patricia Gomez and how he once threw a rock through a neighbor's window. He was sorry about the broken window, he told the tape recorder, and then whispered, "I want to make out with you, Patricia." When he played that last part back, a chill ran up and down his back. He erased his private thoughts.

One morning he and his *carnal* Alex Garcia were sitting on the fender of Rudy's father's 1966 Chevy Malibu. His father kept the Malibu for sentimental reasons and had promised it to Rudy when he turned seventeen, provided he cut the lawn every Saturday and stayed out of gangs.

"Aren't you tired of that stupid thing?" Alex asked, meaning the tape recorder.

"I'm a *barrio* spy," Rudy whispered.

"Get over it," Alex said, sneering.

Rudy might have gotten over it, except that his father called him from the front porch, "Rudy, *ven acá!*"

"Dad, I cut the lawn yesterday," Rudy said. He jumped from the car fender and raked his palm across the lawn, which still glittered with morning dew.

"It's not about the lawn."

Rudy's father worked as a welder and was built for that work, short and strong, with hands as tough as wrenches. His hair was black, though his mustache sprouted a few wiry white hairs. "We're going down to the gym. You want to come, Alex?" He went back inside, the screen door slapping behind him.

Rudy turned to Alex. "Dad wants me to box."

"Put on the gloves?"

"Yeah."

Rudy didn't like the thought of boxing. His cousin Lalo had once hit him by mistake with a plastic bat right on his nose, and although no blood flowed, the sting had forced tears to his eyes.

"I used to box with my brothers," Alex said, bragging.

"Yeah?"

"Yeah, and we just used socks." Alex curled up his

fingers into fists. "Socks for boxing gloves. It was fun."

Rudy changed into mismatched sweats—an orange sweatshirt with a kangaroo pouch and blue sweatpants—and he and Alex hopped into his father's old Buick Electra, a huge car with real steel and lots of legroom.

"Training is good for you," Rudy's father said. He maneuvered the ancient car like a garbage truck, slowly and with lots of twists of the steering wheel. He said that every boy—and most girls, too—should learn to box for self-defense. "My *papi* taught me."

"You get in a lot of fights, Mr. Herrera?" Alex asked.

"Just a few," he answered. "In fact, I had to fight a dude once because of Rudy's mom."

"Really?" Rudy asked.

"It was down in Fowler, and that guy just couldn't understand that his days were over and it was my time."

Rudy recorded his father's talk, and he planned to record himself boxing. He smiled as he pictured himself jabbing and throwing crisp left hooks. He closed his eyes for a moment and scooted down in the seat, picturing himself with a world-title belt hanging on his waist.

They drove to Beto's Bob-and-Weave Gym just off Tulare Street. The gym was famous for producing two silver-medal Olympic champions, one feather-weight champion named Benny "Hit and Slip" Vasquez, and lots of bloody noses.

His father pulled into the driveway and cut the engine. He was dressed in sweats, too, with a clean dish towel at his side. The dish towel was embroidered with two chickens.

They ventured into the gym, which smelled like a pile of socks. There was one main ring, with ropes and a worn canvas floor, and an array of punching bags—speed bags for light work and a heavy hundred-pound bag to bang with all your strength. On a far wall hung jump ropes.

"Beto!" yelled Rudy's dad.

"Hey, *hombre*," Beto returned. He was a small man, with a balloon of stomach under his gray sweatshirt.

They shook hands, and then Rudy's father presented his son and Alex.

"Good-looking boys," Beto declared, sizing them up. He squeezed Rudy's arms and shoulders. He was always searching for more talent for the Golden Gloves. "Help yourself. Gloves are in the shopping cart."

Beto left them when someone called from the office. The "someone" was a girl about Rudy's age. She was tall and her face was heart shaped. She smiled at him and his heart fluttered.

"Check her out," Rudy whispered to Alex, who

was watching two fighters—one Latino, the other black—thrashing each other.

"What?" Alex said.

"A girl is looking at us."

Alex craned his neck and said, "Where?"

Rudy's father squeezed his son's shoulders. He told him the girl was Beto's daughter, and he had better concentrate on boxing, not girls. "OK, *chamacos,* let's do a little rope work," he said as he prodded the boys away, both of them still looking back at the girl, who seemed to be sizing them up.

The boys and Rudy's dad jumped rope awkwardly. They couldn't get the rhythm right. The ropes slapped against their big feet, almost tripping them. Then the three shadowboxed for a while, imitating some of the other boxers, all young men.

Rudy looked for the girl, but she had gone back into the office. He noticed a boy about his age, perhaps younger, who was working on one of the lighter bags. The boy was small and looked harmless. Rudy told Alex he thought he'd ask the boy to go a few rounds.

"You gonna fight him?" Alex asked. "He's smaller than you."

"Box, not fight," Rudy corrected. "And he isn't that little. I'll go easy on him." With his back to his father, he took out the tape recorder. He flicked the "on" switch and breathed, "I'm at Beto's Gym. This is me boxing. There's a really good-looking girl in the office and I think she likes me."

"You gonna use the tape recorder?" Alex asked.

Rudy flicked the tape recorder off and said, "Turn it on when I tell you." He took off his sweatshirt and turned it the other way so it was backward. That way, if he got hit in the stomach, the tape recorder wouldn't break.

With worried-face Alex in tow, Rudy slowly worked his way in the direction of the boy, who came up to his chin. His shoulders were narrow, not rounded off with muscle, and his face was the face of an angel, not a boxer. Rudy said, "Hi," and started chatting with him. He discovered that his name was Victor, he was twelve years old and went to Sequoia Junior High School. He had been training for six months.

"You want to go a few rounds?" Victor asked.

"Sure," Rudy said, bouncing from foot to foot as he tried to look like he knew what he was doing. "But not too hard, OK? This is my first time here."

Victor crossed himself in the name of the Father, the Son, and the Holy Spirit. Rudy followed suit, hitting himself with his heavy gloves in the face, the stomach, and each arm.

He whispered to Alex, "Turn on the tape recorder." He noticed that the girl had come out of the office and was approaching them in long scissoring steps. He started to jab left, left, left, left—left furiously until Alex told him to slow down.

"I can't turn it on if you're bouncing around like a kangaroo," Alex scolded.

"Sorry."

Alex felt for the switch and flicked it on. He squeezed Rudy's shoulders for encouragement and said, "I'll keep time, champ." He looked down at the scratched face of his watch. He counted out, "Five, four, three, two...box!"

The boys tapped gloves and circled each other, jabbing and testing each other's weaknesses. Victor was smaller but very busy with fancy footwork. Rudy tried to imitate him. He moved his feet, circled, and dipped his shoulder. He felt good. From the corner of his eye, Rudy could see his father, who was watching with hands on hips, the dish towel slung like a diaper over his broad shoulder. His father looked proud.

Then Rudy spied the girl, who suddenly said, "Keep your hands up."

Rudy didn't like that, being told what to do.

"You're looking good," the girl said, her own hands up and balled into fists.

Rudy did like that. He flashed a smile at her. But suddenly a jab hit his nose. His eyes watered and his nose hurt. He threw his own punches but they were deflected, and only one grazed Victor's head. Frustrated, Rudy went wild, even growling like a tiger. He threw roundhouse punches, but none of them landed against his opponent. They only stirred the gym air.

"Time," Alex yelled.

"Good round, Victor," Rudy wheezed, bent over with his hands on his knees. He needed air, even the smelly air of the gym. He had kept his mouth closed during the round. His nose felt plugged, as if someone had stopped up his nostrils with a clothespin.

Now Rudy's father was at his side. He looked like he wanted to give his son some instructions, but he kept quiet. He just took the dish towel from his shoulder and wiped Rudy's red face.

"What's your name?" the girl asked.

Rudy could barely get it out, he was so tired, so brain-dead. "Rudy. And . . . and this is . . . Alex."

"You're doing good," the girl said, complimenting him.

Rudy sucked in a lot of air, swallowed, and said, "Thanks . . . a . . . lot."

The two boys boxed a second round, and this time a warmed-up Victor went methodically from head to stomach, back and forth, each punch light but still heavy enough to slow Rudy down. Rudy felt like turtles were moving his arms—they were so slow and aimless. His throat hurt. His lungs burned, as if he were inhaling flames. Once he managed to connect with a bang against Victor's forehead and throw him back on his heels. But Victor recovered and once again continued hitting Rudy with punches that didn't really hurt. They were more bothersome.

"Time," Alex shouted a second time.

Rudy sat down on the floor, his chest heaving.

"You know it's not good to sit down," the girl said cheerfully.

Rudy ignored her. He swallowed and felt the flames in his lungs slowly cool. He took the dish towel and blew his nose. He looked at the *mocos,* expecting flecks of blood, but he found none. He looked over at Victor, who was bouncing from foot to foot, not in the least exhausted.

"I'll get it together now," Rudy said under his breath. He rose to his feet, legs slightly wobbly like the legs of a restaurant table. Then he said out loud, "You got nice punches."

Victor shrugged off the compliment. He said, "One more round."

Rudy looked at Alex, his eyes begging. He looked at the girl and wished she wasn't there.

"Get ready," Alex said, then shouted, "Box!"

Rudy circled Victor, trying to stay away while keeping up the appearance of fearlessness. After all, the kid only came up to his chin. Plus his father was looking on, and so was his best friend, and the girl.

"Hands up, *mi'jo.* Lookin' better!"

Rudy flicked punches, flicked and got out of the

way. Now and then he took a shot. The third round was going his way. He looked good, so good that he began to bob and weave like a pro, a careless mistake. Victor connected with a stiff jab to Rudy's stomach. Rudy groaned, and his arms sagged. Suddenly the round wasn't going his way anymore. He was tired, out of breath, and thirsty—his mind dreamed up a Big Gulp with plenty of ice. He looked over at Alex and pleaded with his eyes to hurry up the time. His lungs burned and his face was hot as a crab in boiling water.

"Go, Rudy! Come on! You can do it!" the girl shouted.

Yeah, sure, Rudy thought, ready to collapse.

Victor connected with a hook to the ribs, which pushed out what remained of the air circulating in Rudy's lungs. He crumpled to his left knee, then his right. Then the pain slowly blossomed. Rudy thought, Oh, what the heck, and fell face foward, the tape recorder bouncing from the pouch of his sweatshirt. He wasn't so much hurt as exhausted. He needed to lie down for a moment. With eyes closed, he pictured Chuy Sanchez, the soldier who never made it back home. He wondered if he would make it back home. When he rolled over and opened his eyes, he saw Alex and the girl standing over him.

"You almost had him," the girl said. "But my brother's pretty tough."

"Her brother," Rudy groaned to himself.

Alex quickly picked up the tape recorder and, although there were fifteen seconds to go, called as loud as he could, "TIME!" The word echoed through the gym. A few of the other boxers stopped. They gazed over at the two boys and then continued their own thrashing.

Rudy's father let his son lie there for a second before he said, "Just like your *papi*—a real fighter!"

After that Rudy sat on a bench, drinking paper cups of water. He was tired and admitted to himself that he was no good at boxing. He admitted that he had liked the girl when he first saw her, but now she embarrassed him. He wished that she would go away, but she kept hammering boxing tips at him.

"Don't drink too much water," she told him.

Rudy crushed the paper cup and hurled it at the mouth of the garbage can.

That night in bed, after a hot bath, Rudy played back the tape recording. First he heard the shuffling of feet on the gym floor and soon gloves glancing off shoulders. Then he heard the first crunch to his nose, which sounded like the noise you make when you step on a snail. He heard his tired breathing and more blows, all smacking, he knew, on target—his face, ribs, stomach. With each smack, he winced as he relived the tiny blows from the tiny kid.

"The kid was tough," he whispered, and laughed to himself in bed.

He listened to the first two rounds and then the final round. He was fascinated, even though he knew what was coming. He covered up his stomach, but the blow on the tape recorder still got through to him. He relived the fall from the heavy, picture-perfect rib shot. He heard the wind gush from his mouth, then the sound of his body as it dropped with a thud to the floor. Rudy was sweating just listening to the recording, and his arms were exhausted. At least I have my brains, he told himself, and the memory of the girl yelling out instructions. It was better than nothing. He knocked a knuckle against his forehead. He touched his ribs, which were sore, and like a floored boxer, one who could not rise, stared up at the lights.

YOUR TURN, NORMA

With ten minutes remaining in class, Norma Lucero first pretended to burp the baby doll on her shoulder, then ran her fingers through her straw-rough hair, and finally worked her pudgy arms back and forth. The doll appeared to move—left arm, then right, left again, right again. She tossed the baby in the air, not too high. She cradled the doll and wanted to hug her, but she didn't want her classmates to see her. She placed the doll on her knee.

"I'll take care of you," Norma cooed at the doll, Amber—named after a girl she had read about in the newspaper. That Amber had died of leukemia in Maryland, a state which most of the students pronounced as "Marilyn."

"Thank you," she said for the doll, her lips barely moving.

Norma gazed around the room, careful not to let

others see that she was talking to the doll. She continued: "If someone hurts you, I'll get them."

"Please don't let them get me," the doll whispered. Her arms were working back and forth as if she were running, a common occurrence at Sequoia Junior High, where every afternoon there were fights that drew blood and anger bitter as pennies. Norma giggled, feeling childish.

One of Amber's eyes wouldn't stay open. Norma pushed it open and a blue eye stared at her, a dead eye, badly scratched, wobbling in its socket. When she let go of the lid, it fell closed. The words *"mal ojo"* were scrawled in ballpoint on the lid.

But Amber's good eye rocked open and closed when Norma tilted her. This eye appeared alert. More than alert, it looked crazed. It looked as if—if the doll were really alive—it would have picked up a pair of scissors and started stabbing. The doll's stare just didn't look right.

"It's your turn, Norma," Mrs. Bledsoe, the teacher, said, heading across the classroom to shush some kids. "Be good to Amber. Remember, she's just like a real baby."

Norma understood. She didn't need to know why it was her turn. Every student in the eighth-grade social studies class had to take care of the baby doll for a week. The message was clear: Get pregnant and you'll carry a baby every day of your teenage life.

Norma got Amber in April. By then Amber was

nearly broken—chipped nose and knee, the eye that wouldn't work, a leg that fell off at the slightest touch. Her dress was tattered, shapeless, the lace collar black from dirty fingers. Some of her shoulder-length hair was gone, revealing holes in her scalp. Behind the holes, there was nothing—just a hollow in her brain area.

"You're all dirty," Norma said. She used spit to rub the words from the eyelid.

Who in this class would get pregnant? Norma wondered. Lucy would because she was dumb. Dorotea and Alicia might because they liked boys more than anything in the world. Carolina would get pregnant because she liked babies. But me, she thought, no way.

Norma stayed away from boys, and most of the *chola* girls, whose faces were caked with makeup—slashes of eyeliner, blue eye shadow, and tattoos on their thumbs and wrists. The girls' baggy pants hid guns, some whispered, blades of every kind, beepers, stolen candies and chips. One day she saw a girl pull a tiny television from her pants pocket. Lots of things went into those pockets, including the hands of groping boys. Norma stayed away from school dances, where girls smoked cigarettes and did their nails in the bathrooms. They primped with tiny mirrors and reread misspelled love letters from boys in juvie.

When the last bell rang at 2:50, Norma gathered

her books into her backpack and shrugged it onto her shoulders. When she left class cuddling baby Amber, some girls raked their fingers through Amber's hair.

"She's getting old," one girl remarked.

"Her nose is all messed up. She been in a fight?" said another, snickering.

Norma smiled but ignored the girls. She intended to clean Amber up. She had a dress that belonged to one of her own dolls, a doll that she had left on a Ferris wheel at the Fresno Fair. She had the clothes, but the doll was gone. Norma pictured it still endlessly riding the Ferris wheel.

As she was leaving the school campus, she ran into Diana Rodriguez, a girl from English class who harassed anyone with good grades.

"You looking at me, nerd?" Diana snarled as she stood above the gutter, her shoes hanging over the edge of the curb. She spat out a mouthful of sunflower shells and hurried over to Norma, both fists closed. Her anger was stoking up a fire in her eyes.

"I'm not looking at you," Norma mumbled. Diana was a gang girl whose lipstick was brown, whose thumbs were marked with tattoos. She wasn't the toughest girl at school, but tough enough to scare most everyone, including the teachers.

"You're looking at me, *estúpida*," Diana sneered.

"No, I'm just going home," Norma said as she turned and started walking away.

"You think you're better than us," Diana demanded hotly.

Diana followed Norma, palming her back, pushing her, calling her names. And with each push, Norma gripped the doll. I won't let them get you, Norma thought. She looked down at the doll's face. One eye was closed and the other, it seemed to her, looked up in terror.

"You think you're so special," Diana yelled.

"I never said that," Norma muttered, her back to Diana.

"You lie, nerd girl."

Diana pulled on her backpack so that Norma stumbled backward in a stutter step. The doll flew out of her hands, its loose leg coming off, the bad eye suddenly opening up. Norma landed on her elbow, a spark of pain shooting up her arm. She winced, one eye closed, the other looking down at the sidewalk. She curled herself into a ball, waiting for Diana to kick her. She didn't.

"Get up!" Diana scolded her as she circled.

"Leave me alone," Norma cried from the ground. When she looked up, Diana was holding the doll's leg like a drumstick. Norma sat up, her backpack slipping off her shoulders. Her elbow hurt. Pebbles were embedded in her palms.

"Let me have the leg," Norma asked, raising her hand.

"Forget you!"

"Please!"

"You want it?"

Norma nodded.

"Then get it from me."

Norma got up but didn't make a move.

"Is this your little doll's *pata*?" Diana taunted. She pushed it in front of Norma's face.

"Ah, leave the girl alone," said Sara, one of Diana's girls. Norma had known Sara since kindergarten. Back then Sara loved to finger paint, and she clapped when they sang. She'd held Norma's hand once when they shared animal crackers. Sara was nice then. Now she was a *chola,* the kindergarten years lost in the past.

"Please," Norma begged, a hand outstretched. "I never done nothing to you."

Diana clicked her tongue at Norma. She turned away, her gang of friends following. Their baggy pants fluttered as they sauntered off.

Norma would have told her father what happened, but he worked on the night shift at the cotton gin. Instead, she told her mother. Her mother had her own complaints. She was tired from working at the dry cleaner's, where the stench of chemicals hung about like a fog. She felt sick from the vapors of the cleaning solution. She was sick from standing up. She was sick from the heat that blasted her eight hours a day.

"Just ask her real nice," her mother muttered from the couch. "If you be nice, then they act nice back."

"It's not like that, Mom."

Her mother thought about it for a moment.

"What's it like, then, *mi'ja?*" she asked.

Norma didn't try to explain. Instead, she told her mother that it was her turn to carry baby Amber.

"That's nice," her mother said weakly.

Norma hurried to her room to get Amber.

"See," Norma said brightly. She held up the doll with one leg.

"That's really nice," her mother repeated, barely audible.

Mom doesn't understand, Norma told herself.

After her own bath, Norma bathed Amber, the water sucking loudly into the leg hole when she dipped her into the washbasin. Bubbles gurgled as Norma submerged Amber in the soapy water. The doll's one good eye looked at Norma as she lay on the bottom of the basin, her hair waving about like seaweed. Norma kept Amber under water for a long time and wondered, as a bubble rose from the doll's eye, how long a real person could hold his breath. She felt spooked, and quickly brought the doll up from the water.

"We'll get it back," she cooed to Amber. She pushed open the dead eye, and it stared at her through a lens of soapy water. Afterward she changed Amber's clothes, slipping her plastic arms into the jumper that had belonged to the doll left on the Ferris wheel. Then she climbed into bed, Amber next to her. She pressed Amber's good eye closed, then turned off the lamp and closed her own eyes.

The next morning Norma stopped the vice principal in the hallway to tell him about Diana Rodriguez stealing Amber's leg.

"I don't have time now," he said. He was hurrying, muttering into his walkie-talkie. Keys jingled like music in his pocket.

Norma repeated that Diana Rodriguez had stolen Amber's leg. "Listen, please," she begged, trying to keep up, her shoulder clipping other kids in the hallway.

But the vice principal didn't hear anything. His mouth at the walkie-talkie, he instructed the person on the other end: "Keep the kid there."

Later rumors abounded. Jesús Lopez had brought a knife to school and had knifed *himself* in a game called Siren. He had tossed the knife into the air, called "Siren!" but didn't scramble out of the way. He stood there, and the knife punched through the top of his ear. It quivered there like a feather.

During lunch Norma spotted Diana Rodriguez. She was walking with her crowd, all gathered together like crows, their eyes sharp as flint. Norma followed her from a safe distance. She saw that Diana didn't carry a purse. She was left-handed and covered up her mouth when she laughed.

"I won't let them get you," Norma said to Amber, her thumb hooked in the hole where Amber's leg had been.

Norma avoided Diana. She avoided everyone, eating her lunch in a rush like a squirrel. In social studies she tried to tell Mrs. Bledsoe, but the teacher was busy warning two boys to settle down. They had propped pens behind their ears and said that they were Jesús Lopez.

"That's not funny at all!" Mrs. Bledsoe scolded. "And you, Norma, put your hand down!"

"Her leg is gone," Norma said over the noise of the classroom. "Diana Rodriguez stole it!"

No one listened.

Or so she thought. But later someone told Diana that Norma had snitched on her.

"I'm going to get you!" Diana threatened her in the hallway. She would have gotten Norma then, except Sara held her back. "Wait till after school."

Norma cut her last class, fleeing with Amber. She rushed home and hid in her house. Norma turned on the television and watched afternoon cartoons. Her heart slowed, and her arms lay limp, her fingers holding a pencil. She sat with her binder open, occasionally looking down at her math homework.

At five-thirty her mother came home, pushing

open the door with her shoulder. She was tired, eyes half closed in exhaustion.

"You want some water, Mom?" Norma asked, getting up.

"Thank you, *mi'ja,*" her mother said, sitting down on the sofa next to the doll, which she picked up.

"Where did you find her?" her mother asked when Norma came back into the room, walking slowly. She had poured too much water into the glass.

"What?"

"Your doll," she said, patting Amber's belly. "Didn't you lose her at the fair?"

Norma told her mother that that doll was lost for good and that the one she was holding was baby Amber.

"I'm supposed to take care of her," Norma said. She didn't explain that the doll was meant to show girls how their lives would change if they became pregnant.

Her mother put the doll down and sipped at the glass of water, her mouth puckered around the rim.

"Mom, Diana's going to get me."

She told her mother how Diana had stolen Amber's leg.

"Just be nice to this girl," her mother said, "and she'll be nice to you." Then her head turned slowly to the flashes of light from the television.

Norma cried in bed that night. The next day she

woke very early to sunlight stabbing like a spear across the floor. She made hot chocolate and looked in her parents' bedroom—her mother was a small lump next to her father, who was a camel hump in the bed. He had come home late, as usual, and crawled into bed. When her father rolled over, Norma tiptoed away, returning to the kitchen, and sipped her hot chocolate.

She dressed quickly and made a sandwich, pouring Fritos into a paper bag. Then her mother appeared in the doorway of the kitchen. She tied her robe and took a few shuffling steps in her worn slippers. Her face was pressed with a mesh of wrinkles.

"What are you doing?" her mother asked sleepily.

"I have to be at school early," Norma lied. "It's a test I got to take."

She had to get to school early in order to avoid Diana and her gang. She even took a different route, always glancing around, nervous. She stopped when she saw some men shoving shopping carts piled with cans and glass. Instead of walking down Cedar Avenue, she cut down an alley and through small dusty streets, where occasionally she heard a city rooster crow. Dogs barked as she passed, and some leaped halfway up the fences, frightening her.

Because the school was still locked, Norma climbed the fence and walked over the dewy grass, leaving a caravan of footprints. She sat on a bench near the backstop. There was no one there, not even the janitors with bundles of keys chiming on their leather belts. The sun began to flare over the school building, its orangish fire splashing against the trees. Only then did the campus look beautiful.

"I wish I was rich," Norma muttered. "I wouldn't have to go here."

She took Amber out of her backpack. She had had her for three days, and in those few days the doll had gotten more beaten up. Norma felt beaten up, too. That morning she couldn't promise Amber that no one would hurt her. She couldn't make promises to herself, either. She knew that Diana would get her eventually.

Norma set Amber on the bench and then pushed her hand back into the backpack. To give herself strength, she brought out her lunch and devoured it. She wiggled her fingers, which were powdered with salt from the Fritos. Then the fingers went into her mouth for a quick lick. Now there is nothing to look forward to, Norma thought.

Norma got through most of her classes, but during the last break, just before social studies, Diana sneaked up on her while she was coming out of the girls' rest room. Norma ran and Diana chased after her, finally catching her near one of the soccer goals, its spidery net chewed with holes.

"You squealed on me!" Diana snarled.

"I didn't," Norma cried.

"You lie, girl."

Diana pulled Norma's hair, and Norma, not knowing what to do, pulled Diana's hair. She was surprised by her strength. She was surprised that Diana groaned from the pain. She pulled harder, loosening a snatch of hair. When Diana released her hair, Norma did the same.

"Oooooo," the ring of onlookers shouted. "Get her, Diana."

"I didn't mean to," Norma cried. She felt like running, but she stayed there, cradling Amber, whose stare was fixed on the sky. The kissing O of the doll's mouth was bloodless, the painted-on lip color long gone.

Diana was all over Norma, slapping and scratching. With her one free hand, Norma scratched back. Then she let Amber fall and scratched with both hands. She grabbed the entire flower of Diana's ear and pulled with all her strength. Diana screamed.

"I'm sorry," Norma said, looking down at her palms, where an earring lay like a fishing lure. A bead of blood hung on to the post.

"You're dead, girl," Diana sniveled.

The girls parted, both breathing hard.

"What did I do?" Norma cried, snot running from her nose. She held her palm stretched out, gesturing for Diana to take the earring.

But Diana slapped it away and jumped on Norma, riding her back and punching. Norma shook her off, but Diana was on her again. Norma began to weaken. Diana punched her in the eye, and she saw a flash like a firecracker exploding.

"I didn't do nothing," Norma repeated, stepping back with a hand over her eye, a ribbon of drool dangling from her mouth. Then she dropped to her knees and curled herself into a ball. She was only kicked twice before the vice principal stopped the beating. Diana tried to punch the vice principal, but he squeezed her neck until her shoulders rose in pain.

"Don't you even think about it, girl," he said fiercely. He led Diana away and said to Norma, "You, go to the nurse's office."

Norma rose slowly, picked up Amber, and gathered her books and notebooks, which had scattered from her backpack.

"You did good, Norma," someone said as Norma walked slowly, painfully, to the nurse's office. When she got there, her eye was swollen and her back hurt. She kept pressing a palm to her nose to see if she was bleeding, but the moisture ran clear.

"What happened to you?" the nurse's assistant said as she headed out the door.

"Diana Rodriguez got me," Norma said.

The woman pointed to a seat and told her not to fool around. The nurse would see her in a moment. Then she left.

Norma sat quietly while someone cried "Ow" behind the closed door. It was a boy's voice, and his shout saddened her.

"They got us," she said to Amber, who, she noticed, now had both eyes closed. She peeled them open, but they both dropped. Not even the doll wanted to see Norma's wounded face. Norma sat still. She looked at the poster of a polar bear climbing on top of an iceberg. She looked at the calendar next to it. It was April, and there were two months of school left, plenty of time for more trips to the nurse's office.

"I'm going to call your mom," a voice said behind the door. "Now go take a seat."

The door opened with a click. Jesús came out, his ear newly bandaged. He took a seat without looking at Norma, who touched her own ear and wondered what kind of pain arose from such a stabbing.

"How long do you get to keep the baby?" he asked after a while.

"For a week," she said. "This is my third day." She looked at Jesús's bandaged ear, then asked, "How come you stuck yourself?"

"José did it," Jesús said.

He explained that it was his knife, but José had thrown it into the air. He looked down at his shoes. Sniffling, he gazed up, touched the doll's hair, and asked, "Where's the leg?"

Norma turned her face to the polar bear forever

caught on an iceberg. She started crying, her shoulders jerking up and down. She wiped her nose on her hand and stopped crying just long enough to tell Jesús that Diana had stolen it and that now both eyes wouldn't open.

"And look at *my* eye," Norma said, feeling it tenderly with a finger. It was nearly swollen shut.

Jesús stared at it, his mouth falling open.

"I got an eye like that one time," he said in a whisper. "It takes a week to be good again."

The two remained quiet. Norma let Amber, dirty with grass stains, lie in her lap, facedown, as if she were about to spank her for being a naughty child. The nurse called her from the other room.

"It don't hurt," Jesús said.

"Huh?"

"What they do to you," Jesús said, kicking the floor with his shoe.

Norma got up, hugging Amber, and went into the office to see what they do to you when one eye won't work.

THE FUNERAL SUITS

Tomás Mejia stepped out of line at the post office when he recognized a neighbor's face hanging on a clipboard on the wall. He stared at the picture: James A. Dragwell II, wanted for theft of U.S. mail. The guy's face was stern and creased, with eyebrows like pads of steel wool. A huge lump poked from his throat like a doorknob. His nose looked like a root pulled from contaminated earth. He looked evil.

"*Hijole.*" Tomás whistled. He remembered that his dad had lent this guy their jumper cables. He remembered that he had seen this man in their backyard! When he and his older cousin Miguel, their shirtless bodies wet from the quick-trigger blasts of squirt guns, had asked him what he was doing, he had said that his cat was lost.

That was the day the laundry had disappeared from the clothesline. Their jeans and pants, their

Fresno State Bulldog sweatshirts, the T-shirts with an array of sayings. Even their underwear—their *chones*—had disappeared, which saddened his mother, who'd said it is a dark day when underwear is stolen.

Tomás got back into line and bought one stamp. He licked the stamp and pounded it on the PG&E bill. His mother—ever money conscious, a saver of crushed aluminum cans and clipped coupons—bought stamps only when she needed them.

As he left the post office, he looked once more at James A. Dragwell II. The man definitely deserves to be there, he thought to himself. Tomás then rifled through the rest of the criminals on the clipboard—all ugly, dangerous, and wanted, it seemed, for something called "fraud." He made a mental note to ask his dad what that meant.

When a postal worker came out of the office, Tomás stopped him and said, "I know that man."

"What?" the worker asked, heaving a sack of mail onto his shoulders. "What you say?" he asked a second time, his voice as deep as a canal frog.

"Him," he repeated. He pointed at the clipboard.

The postal worker stopped to examine the face. "He looks like my brother-in-law," he commented, and walked away, indifferent.

Tomás hurried home, but before he could shout about what he had learned, his mother asked if he mailed the letter.

"Yeah."

"Did you put the stamp on right?" she asked. She was holding the hose of their vacuum cleaner. A clot of hair was pinched in her fingers.

"I licked it with my spit," he said. Then his voice rose. "Mom, our neighbor is a criminal. What's 'fraud'?"

"What are you talking about?" she asked, frowning.

He explained what he had seen.

His mother sat down, the clot of hair still in her hands. She passed it to Tomás, who went into the kitchen and dropped it in the garbage bag under the sink.

"You mean the man with the tattoo?" she asked.

Tomás remembered the skull tattoo. The skull had a smoldering cigarette between its dicelike teeth.

"That's the one," Tomás said. "He's wanted for stealing mail. What does 'fraud' mean?"

"It means...," his mother started to say, then stopped. "It means that you are no good." She rose to her tired feet and turned on the vacuum, which howled like a hundred dogs stuck in one room.

Tomás left the house. He stood on the front lawn and looked across the street to where James A. Dragwell II had lived. He had gone, dragging along his family, a wife with insanely cut hair and three kids, each as round as Humpty-Dumpty. Since then the house had been abandoned. The grass grew tall and the weeds scraggly. The porch was a graveyard for yellowed newspapers. One window was broken and the antenna on the roof had collapsed. Even the oil-splotched driveway had begun to grow tufts of grass between its cracks.

Tomás walked across the street and peered into the living-room window. A couch with its guts spilling out stood in the living room. There was a can of uncovered paint sitting on a newspaper.

We could have been killed, Tomás thought. His heart pounded. I know a criminal, he thought. He knew that petty crimes led to larger crimes, and while he didn't know much about snatching other people's mail, he knew that stealing might lead to beating people up and perhaps even murder. There was a definite connection in Tomás's mind.

It was summer. No wind stirred the trees. Time was a slow cat walking across the hot lawn.

There wasn't much to do. Tomás decided to go tell his friend Larry, a kid up the street, about the criminal they both had known. Larry was twelve, two years older than Tomás, and clever enough to know how to bang soda machines for free drinks. His house was messy, almost like James A. Dragwell's house. Except, now and then, a sprinkler was set on the lawn to twirl out tears of water. Larry lived with his mother and two dogs, both with snipped tails.

On the way over, he snatched apricots from Señor Lara's yard and felt not the least bit guilty because so many lay on the ground, buzzing with gnats and flies.

Tomás stopped in his tracks when he saw a cop car in front of Larry's house. Apricot juice ran from his chin and fingers. He tried to size up the meaning of the cop's car. A glare bounced off the chrome bumpers. He hurried toward the house, his mouth chomping the last of the fruit. On the porch he raised a hand to knock, but pulled away because the door opened. Out came Larry, his face freckled with tears, and a cop with his huge hand on the back of Larry's neck.

"Larry!" Tomás cried, startled and confused, but stepping out of the way.

Larry didn't say anything. He let his mother do the talking. She came out yelling at him.

"See!" she scolded. Blue curlers were bouncing on the top of her hair. The hair around the curlers was pressed down with bobby pins. "You get smart, and see!"

Tomás's knees felt weak. His mouth, despite the ripe apricot he had just downed, was dry from fear, and felt like a piece of leather. He watched his friend as the cop led him down the porch and into the back of the cop car. Before the car drove away, Tomás rushed down the steps to the car.

"What did you do, Larry?" Tomás asked. His face was pinched with worry.

Larry shrugged his shoulders, then his head jerked

back as the cop's car roared away from the curb, leaving only the stink of exhaust.

"See!" Larry's mother shouted after him. "See what you get for acting so smart!"

Tomás hoped Larry's mother would explain what Larry had done, but she stomped away, her head bouncing wildly with curlers. She stopped and set the sprinkler on the front lawn, then snapped at Tomás, "You'll get yours, too."

"But I didn't do nothing."

"That's what he gets for putting his name all over Roosevelt High!"

So that's it, Tomás thought. Larry got busted tagging walls.

He left feeling that life was uncertain and that at any time you might be picked up and thrown in the back of a cop car.

Back at home Tomás told his mother what had happened to Larry, and she sounded mad when she told him never to play with that boy.

"You're going to get in trouble, too," she scolded.

For a moment Tomás saw his own face hanging on a wanted poster at the post office.

When his dad came home, his pants covered with cement from the job site, his eyebrows powdered white, Tomás told him first about Larry and then about the neighbor whose face he had seen at the post office. "Did he ever give us our jumper cables back?"

"Yes, of course," his father answered, already sitting down in his recliner, which was as gray and huge as an elephant. A glass of iced tea sat on the TV tray. The remote control was in his hand, but the TV was still off.

"Maybe Larry's on the news," Tomás said.

His father laughed. Dust from his eyebrows sprinkled onto his lap. He asked his son for a wet washcloth, and Tomás hurried to the bathroom to rinse one. From there he could hear the TV pop on.

Tomás handed his father the washcloth.

"Dad, you ever steal anything?" Tomás asked.

"Almost never," his father said, his face faintly shiny now. He tossed the washcloth back to Tomás, who sat on the edge of the couch waiting for a full-blown confession.

"What does that mean?"

He chuckled and told his son to go out and cut the lawn, something he liked to say as a joke.

"No, tell me!" Tomás begged.

His father muted the television—the mouths of the news team moved up and down, but no words came out. After he sipped from his iced tea, he told Tomás how he and his brother stole a whole rack of suits.

"You did?"

"We were young, *muchacho,*" he said, reflecting on

the past, his hands folded neatly over his belly. "And we were stupid, because the suits were no good. They came from a mortuary."

His father explained that the back of each suit was cut out to make it easier to dress the deceased. The pants, too—they didn't have any backs.

"No backs?"

His father nodded. He sighed and said that Miguel had kept a couple of the suits for when they died. The clothing for their funerals would be free, he figured. He said that Miguel was keeping them in mothballs at his place.

"Now, go outside and cut the lawn!"

Tomás went outside. There was no one to kick around with until dinner was served, which was always at six o'clock, rain or shine. Then he hurried back inside and, in the secrecy of the hallway, he telephoned his cousin Miguel.

"Yeah, what do you want?" his cousin muttered. Miguel was Larry's age, twelve, but tall as an ostrich and more sullen because his parents had gotten a divorce. He had recently cut his hair—the *pelón* look was in—and was thinking of getting a tattoo on his thumb.

"You know, my dad and yours used to steal," Tomás said.

"Get out of here."

"They stole these clothes from the funeral place."

"What are you talking about, homes? You been sniffing glue?"

Tomás told his cousin that he was serious and that after dinner—Tomás sniffed the air, which was heavy with the smell of *chiles rellenos*—he would bike down to Miguel's house.

"The suits are at your place," Tomás said. He started to say something else, but Miguel hung up.

Tomás rode over to Miguel's house after he ate dinner and helped his mother with the dishes. He found Miguel in his bedroom, sitting in front of a whirling fan and wearing a headset.

"Where's your mom?" Tomás asked.

Miguel didn't hear him. He hooked a thumb, signaling for Tomás to close his bedroom door. Tomás did.

"How can you ride your bike in this heat?" his cousin asked, pulling off his headset.

"It ain't that hot."

Sweat dripped down his face and clung to his T-shirt.

"And what do you mean about the 'funeral place'? You talk weird for a little punk."

Tomás, now sitting on the bed and enjoying the benefit of the fan, said that it was true, that his father and Miguel's father had stolen suits when they were younger. He told his cousin that they had saved one each for their own funerals.

"And listen to this," Tomás yelled over the noise

of the fan. "Larry got picked up by the cops. I was there!"

" 'I was there,' " mimicked Miguel. "You're nowhere, man. You're on glue, homes."

Tomás suggested that they check Miguel's father's closet and Miguel said, "Forget my father. He left Mom, and now we're on our own."

Still, after a few more minutes of haranguing from Tomás, Miguel said, "OK, OK, OK."

Since his mother wasn't home, it was easy for them to rifle through the closet. They pulled at skirts and blouses, sweaters, musty coats, and girdles as stiff as football shoulder pads. Finally, in the back of the closet, they came across two blue suits with their backs gone.

"You're right," Miguel said, holding up the suit. "They got no backs. It's spooky, homes."

He pressed the jacket to his body, then slipped into it, his lanky arms wiggling like snakes into the sleeves.

"This one's too short," he remarked as he took off the jacket. "Gimme the other one."

Tomás handed him the other jacket.

"This one fits," Miguel said, wiggling his arms out. "But it feels weird with no back."

Tomás tried on the other jacket, which was big as a tent on him. Then he felt in the pocket and pulled out a piece of paper with the name *Rafael Gonzalez*.

"*¡Hijole!*" Tomás screamed. "This is my dad's funeral jacket."

Miguel checked his pocket and found the name of his father—Miguel Huerta—on a piece of paper.

Both of them sat on the bed, depressed that their fathers had their funeral clothes ready. They looked at the pants crumpled on the floor.

For Tomás there was no use trying on the pants. But for Miguel, the fit would be perfect, possibly even short. He had grown two inches in two months and towered over Tomás by nearly a foot.

"OK, Einstein," Miguel said. "We got the clothes. Now what?"

"I don't know," Tomás said. "Maybe we should wear them? People might think we're important."

"As long as they just see us from the front," Miguel said, laughing.

Because it was something to do, they slipped into the jackets and wore them outside, laughing like hyenas on the front lawn.

"These *trajes* are hot," Miguel complained.

"Yeah, but we look stylish."

The sun had nearly set, and a mesh of dusk began to take over the day. Porch lights clicked on, and moths as big as human ears began to beat around the lights' orangy glow.

"Hey, let's go down to the playground," Miguel suggested.

The boys left wearing the jackets, both of them giggling because they looked like the Bible people who go up and down the block saving people.

"If you see Cindy," Miguel warned, "be cool."

Tomás looked up at his cousin. He'd never realized how long Miguel's neck was. His friends called him Ostrich and, sure enough, he looked like one.

"You like Cindy, huh?" Tomás asked.

"It's none of your business. Just don't act *estúpido*. And remember: Don't turn around!"

At the playground, Coach Padilla was playing Ping-Pong in front of the rec room and within earshot of the telephone.

"What are you doing in those coats?" Coach asked. He was a college student who had rocks in his shoulders and a stomach as hard as an anvil. He needed those muscles at that playground. "You guys going somewhere?"

"A party," Miguel said coolly.

"You ain't going nowhere." Coach twirled a paddle in his hand, stirring up a breeze meant for his face.

Tomás rolled up the sleeves of his jacket and said to the coach, "In that case, you can't go. That's why we're here. To invite you."

Coach laughed, shook his head, and said to his opponent, "Seventeen–fourteen."

The boys left walking backward, not letting the

coach see that there were no backs to their suits. While they were walking over to the bleachers, where there was a group of girls, Miguel asked about Larry.

"They busted him because he was putting his *placa* all over town."

"Is that all?" Miguel said, clicking his tongue. "I'd be in juvie nineteen times if they caught me."

"Then I saw my neighbor at the post office," Tomás started to say.

But Miguel shushed him. His eyes, the eyes of a fox staring at a chicken coop, were on the girls.

"Hey!" the girls screamed, all of them cheerful because something different was on the horizon.

Tomás hurried his steps, but Miguel slowed to a crawl, not wanting to seem to be excited to see them.

"Where are you going? Where did you get the jackets? Can we come with you?" the girls asked.

"Hey, Cindy," Miguel said in a low voice. Then he couldn't help himself. He smiled a huge smile.

"So what are you guys doing?" Cindy asked. She was holding a Popsicle stick pocked with her teeth marks.

"Going to a party," Miguel lied.

"It's at the White House," Tomás butted in.

Miguel gave him a long look.

"Nah, these *trajes* belong to my dad and Tomás's

dad." He turned around and showed them. "See, they ain't got no backs."

"What happened to the backs?" Cindy asked.

"The jackets are for their funerals," Tomás said. He explained that it was easier to dress people this way before they got buried.

"That's cool," a girl said.

Miguel let the girls admire and touch the jackets. He explained that his jacket was his father's jacket.

"And ole Tommy here's wearing *his* dad's jacket."

Tomás beamed.

But his beaming smile fell like a lamp off an end table when Sleepy and Chino, two genuine *vatos locos,* sauntered around the corner of the bleachers. They were wearing sawed-off Dickies, hair nets, and tank tops that sported the words ¿Y QUÉ? They stopped and sized up the girls, then Miguel and Tomás.

"What's going down here?" Sleepy asked in a slippery voice.

Miguel's neck tightened.

"We're just talking," Miguel whispered.

"Talking? Talking 'bout what?"

Miguel answered, "Stuff." His neck seemed to have shortened.

"What you got to say to my girls?" Sleepy asked.

"We ain't your girls," one of them said. "We don't go out with *cholos.*"

Sleepy ignored the girl with guts and saw that Miguel and Tomás were dressed in jackets.

"*¿Qué pasa con tus trajes?*" he asked. "You doing a spot for Target, *ese?*"

Chino went up to Tomás, who was shaking like a leaf.

"How come you're looking at me, stupid?" he asked, his face hovering near Tomás's face. Tomás could smell the sunflower seeds on his breath.

"I ain't looking at you," Tomás said, his eyes deflating slowly like balloons as his gaze fell to the grass. He thought of James A. Dragwell, whose face was at the post office; then Larry; then his own dad, who had stolen; and now these two. Petty criminals wherever he turned.

Chino pushed Tomás out of the way and approached Miguel.

"Sleepy asked you a question, homeboy," Chino slurred. "What you doing with jackets? Going to a party?"

Miguel swallowed and stayed quiet.

"Speak English," Chino hissed.

"Show some *respeto*," Sleepy said. "Answer his question why you're not answering me, *ese.*"

Sleepy was now up in Miguel's face.

"Take off those jackets," Sleepy demanded.

The two boys were out of them in a flash.

"How come the backs are gone?" Chino asked.

Miguel and Tomás shrugged their shoulders.

Then Miguel brightened up and said, "They're for the summer. You know, so your back don't sweat."

Sleepy said that was stupid, but Chino liked the jackets.

"Put them on us," Chino said.

Tomás fitted Chino, and Miguel fitted Sleepy.

"You guys look good," Miguel said, risking a compliment.

"Did I tell you to talk?" Sleepy asked. "First you don't want to talk and now you're talking up. Shaddup."

The girls started to leave, one by one, all of them drifting toward the bright halogen lights of the rec room. While Miguel wanted to look up at Cindy, he kept his gaze on the ground. He knew when to be quiet.

"They look sharp, but they feel weird without no backs," Chino said.

"You can have them," Tomás volunteered.

"Don't tell us what we can or can't have," Chino said. He hooked a finger under Tomás's chin and nearly lifted him up. Tomás's eyes grew as big as a bloated bullfrog's.

"They're gifts," Miguel offered.

"Shaddup!" Sleepy shouted, his hands closing into fists. "I'm in such a good mood that I don't hear your voice. *¿Entiendes?*"

Miguel fell quiet.

"We look all *suave*," said Chino, and slapped Sleepy's outstretched hands in a low five.

"You really look like fashion models," Tomás added, then slapped a hand across his mouth.

"I'm going to smack you one!" Sleepy barked. To Chino he asked, "Should we beat 'em up?"

Chino thought for a moment and then concluded, "Nah, we'll let them go today, but tomorrow, *pues, quién sabe.*"

While Tomás and Miguel stood in the creeping darkness, the *vatos locos* walked slowly away, their heads directed toward the future, and their bodies already half dressed for their funerals.

LITTLE SCAMS

Mario's little scams on the world had started a year ago when he was thirteen. He and his friend Tony, a glue sniffer, were eating a bag of pork rinds they'd snatched from Hanoian's Market. They had asked the manager for cardboard boxes, and as Tony pretended to juggle the boxes, Mario snatched three bags of pork rinds off a metal tree and let them drop into a box. They returned home and sat in the living room with the TV on. They ate pork rinds, a blast of moist air from the cooler flicking their hair about. They thought they were smart and went over and over how they'd juggled the boxes like clowns.

"I got an idea, homes," Mario said after a while. "Stop eating."

"What?" Tony asked, but not immediately because it took time for ideas to sink into his head.

"We're going to get our money back." Mario

waved a hand at the pork rinds, or *chicharrones,* as they called them.

Tony swallowed. "But we stole 'em. They ain't going to give us money back for something we stole."

Mario didn't bother to explain. He got up with a hopeful spring in his step and went outside to the garage. The week before his mother had smoked out a wasps' nest, and the wasps had blown away in an angry cloud. He searched the cement floor for a few dead wasps, scooped them up with his bare hand, tossed them in the one uneaten bag, and took it back to Hanoian's for a refund.

"You got bees in your *chicharrones,*" Mario ranted to the first person he saw in a store apron. "I don't eat bees!"

The box boy peered into the bag of pork rinds, and so did a checker on break, a curl of cigarette smoke unraveling from his nostrils. The manager, wearing a crooked bow tie, came to see the commotion. His mustache twitched.

"The kid says there were bugs in his potato chips," the checker explained to the manager, whose name, Jerry, was embroidered on his apron.

"*Chicharrones,*" Tony corrected.

"Bugs?" the manager asked as he put on his glasses. He told the box boy to cup his hands and then let the contents pour into them. Out rattled the pork rinds, broken and curled like orange peels.

Then the dead wasps appeared, brittle as parchment.

"Good god!" the manager cried. He held up a wasp stiff as a leaf.

That was how Mario got $1.49, the first of his scams. He tried another store and then another, all with success. Sometimes he and Tony used wasps in the potato chip and pork rind bags, and other times they dropped in other insects—cockroaches, daddy longlegs, red ants, potato bugs, and powdery moths that had battered themselves to death against porch lights. They tried other odd things, too—a bird's wing, dead flowers, and rusty bottle caps.

"How about this?" Tony said one time. He held up a Tic Tac box he picked up from the gutter.

"You're stupid, dude," Mario said, and laughed. He flung the box like a rock.

But their scams stopped when the manager from Hanoian's, the guy with the twitching mustache, happened to work one day at the Hanoian's Market across town. Mario was thrusting a bag of barbecue potato chips at one of the clerks there. Mario and Tony were complaining loudly, stabbing their fingers at the box boy, a kid just older than they were.

"I know you boys," the manager said, eyeing Mario and Tony. He looked around frantically, his face reddening. He had sized up their scheme. "Harold! Harold, get the door."

Mario and Tony ran with the manager on their tails. Mario snagged a whole pie from someone's cart as he ran past. He figured that he was already in trouble, and if they got away, they'd have something to bend around their sweet tooth. If they got caught, they would just throw the pie down.

They caught Tony, but the homeboy played dumb, an easy role for him, and shrugged his shoulders.

"Who's your friend?" a cop asked.

Tony shrugged his shoulders again.

"What school do you go to? How old are you?" a second cop asked, his mustache jumping up and down.

"Are you from Mexico?" the first cop asked in Spanish, then in English.

Tony shrugged to every question, shrugged like a boxer warding off blows. He finally said with a slur, "I don't know nothing."

He went to juvie for a week, and when he got out, his mother sent him away to live with his father in Merced.

Mario continued with his scams on his own. He swindled his five-year-old neighbor. Mario held out a handful of pennies and told him they were worth more than the tooth-fairy's dollar.

"Look at how many there are!" Mario crowed. He jiggled forty-three pennies in his cupped hands. "There are hundreds!" But it was a piece of cake to fool a five-year-old. Mario preferred a bigger challenge.

So he put an old price tag on a nearly empty bottle

of shampoo and took it back to Safeway for an exchange. He simply filled it with water and some goo his mother kept under the sink. He did this twice, each time complaining that the shampoo made his hair stink. It worked like a charm. Mario was determined to scam the world, make it pay. He even stole his uncle's calling card to phone Tony in Merced. But Tony, high on glue, didn't have much to say and slurred most of his words. Mario did understand when Tony mumbled, "It's hot here, just like there. I wanna go to Alaska."

Mario figured out a profitable scam when his mother hauled him to the Goodwill store on Ventura Avenue. She wanted him to try on some dress-up shoes. They had been invited to her cousin's daughter's wedding in Dinuba.

"I don't want to go to some *estúpido* wedding," Mario snapped. He sucked in the air in the shoe section. "This place is *fuchi*. It smells like—"

His mother didn't let him complete his sentence.

"You're going, and that's all there is to it," she growled. Mario's mother was small, almost kid sized, but her face was pleated with wrinkles carved from years of smoking.

"How come I can't wear my Nikes?"

Mario's mother ignored him. She picked up pairs of shoes, one set after another, and looked for holes. Then she looked at the laces. Some of them were frayed like candlewicks, others were black from dragging through gutters. But mostly she looked for the price, for something under six dollars plus the rattling change in her purse.

Mario got an idea when he was squirming into a pair of butter-colored shoes, the kind that John Travolta might have worn in the 1970s. He looked out the window and saw clothes, appliances, furniture, and things set out in front of the Goodwill truck. The old guy taking donations was sitting in one of the chairs, a newspaper folded on his lap.

I'll come back, Mario thought. His mind turned like a raffle cage, turned and came up with another scam, which would have to wait.

Mario did go to the wedding, and what excited him more than the cake, the hordes of girls his age, the *mariachis,* the free sodas in tubs of icy water, and the chicken *mole,* was the bride dancing. The bride was Hermelinda, a name he kept forgetting.

"What's her name again?" Mario asked.

"Hermelinda," her mother said, her face lost in a wafer of cigarette smoke. "How many times do I have to tell you?"

Mario watched Hermelinda as she took to the dance floor, and the men, one after another, came up and pinned money to her gown, or simply pressed tens and twenties in her palms. The bills fluttered in the twirling of her one-two-three, one-two-three waltz.

Mario had never seen so much money. He never had such an opportunity to make some of it his. He pictured his wallet packed with bills, greasy dollars that had been fingered and thumbed through time.

"I'm going to dance with her," Mario said to his mother, who was talking with her *comadre*. Both of their faces were lost in a haze of cigarette smoke.

"Pórtate bien," Mario's mother said. She snapped open her large purse, and it fell open like the jaws of an alligator. She pushed her hand into its mouth, fiddled, and brought out five dollars. She handed it to Mario without explaining. He walked away from his mother and then pushed the five dollars into his pocket.

"Life's sweet," he told himself. He waited for the song to end and a new one to start.

When "These Eyes" started to blare from the speakers, Mario approached the bride. She turned and opened her arms to accept him, and for a moment he imagined himself in a movie.

"I never did this before," he said, smiling. He liked her, the perfume she gave off, her hair, her teeth, square and white. But he liked all the money she wore best.

"It's a first for me, too," she said. Then she added almost rudely, "Just don't step on my hem."

He smiled at her, met her eyes, and then as she swallowed him up in her arms, their bodies turning to a slow song, his eyes fell on a twenty, handsomely twisted into the shape of a bow tie and pinned to her veil. He looked at five- and ten-dollar bills, the faces of dead presidents smirking at him. He held the bride and slowly, carefully, he unpinned the twenty. Then he let go of her and the next dancer approached her.

He hurried away, hands cupped around the twenty. He stood by the cake, bright as a dollhouse, and admired the bride. She smiled at some dude across the floor.

Mario came out ahead at the wedding, but he thought his next little scam would be even more profitable. On that Monday he returned to the Goodwill store and stood some distance away in the parking lot of a closed meat market. He clutched the red plastic handle of a shopping cart. The sun blazed on his back; sweat crawled like ants on his face.

"Get up! Leave!" he muttered to himself, to the old man, who was sitting on a bar stool and listening to a baseball game on the radio. Finally he did, when the clerk from the store called.

"It's Jenny," the clerk hollered.

"Who?" the old man asked, standing up. He fiddled with the crotch of his pants.

"Jenny!" the clerk yelled, stepping from the store,

an age-peppered hand shading her eyes from the sun. The old man moved like a spider.

Before the old man was in the store, Mario advanced, as quick as a fox, jumping a small cement-block fence and racing to the truck. He boosted himself up and discovered shadows and dead, dusty air. He saw plastic garbage bags of clothes, but what caught his eye were a vacuum cleaner, a stroller, and a video game. Swiftly he brought each down and hauled them away—his hands carrying the large items, his grinning teeth clamped down on the cord of the video game. He set these things in the shopping cart and wiped his sweaty face. He was breathing hard and his hands were trembling like squirrels.

"I ain't scared," he told himself.

He turned to see if the old man had returned to his place at the mouth of the truck. He hadn't. The area around the truck was quiet in the afternoon sun. A car drove down the street, followed by another. But the place appeared deserted, off-limits.

Mario jumped the fence and raced back. He climbed into the truck. He searched wildly about for things that might sell. His eyes fell on the golf clubs, and although he couldn't judge their quality, he knew that they were easier to carry than the portable TV half hidden behind a cardboard box of clothes. He hugged the clubs in his arms and descended the ladder. Then he scrambled back up and got the TV.

"What are you doing?" the old man cried, shuffling toward the truck.

Mario jumped.

"I'm getting my clubs," Mario lied to the man.

"What?" the old man asked.

"My mom left them by accident," Mario lied again as he started to escape. He looked down at the TV in his hands. He added: "And the TV. It was an accident. My mom is in Alaska now, but she left these things here. She was in a hurry."

Mario babbled as he hurried away, shouting, "She left these things here because my uncle is in Alaska." He was incoherent, making no sense, but he believed his words. He believed that the clubs were his, that he had spent hours watching TV from the portable in his hands.

"What are you talking about?" the old man asked.

"My mother left," he shouted, not looking back. "She's in Alaska and I ain't got to tell you. My uncle died of cancer watching TV."

Mario hurried away. He tossed the clubs over the fence and then balanced the TV on his shoulder. He climbed over and looked back at the old man, who was standing in the heat with his hands on his hips.

With everything piled in the cart, Mario pushed away like a pirate.

The next day he took his loot over to his *abuelita* Carmen's house, where he planned a yard sale.

"Where did you get all this?" his *abuelita* asked. Her hand waved about like a wand over the things spread out on her lawn.

"From Tony," Mario answered.

"Who's Tony?" she asked.

"He had to move to Alaska," Mario said. "His uncle has cancer, and Tony wanted to see him before he dies."

His *abuelita* held up a golf club. "Not many Mexican kids play golf."

"His uncle did," Mario answered. He licked his lips. "They belonged to him, and the cancer chewed off his arms."

Mario's grandmother shook her head. She went back inside, and spied on her grandson from the living-room window. She watched him for a long minute and then pulled the curtain closed on his yard sale.

"She don't trust me, my own grandmother," Mario muttered to himself. "Forget her!"

In his head he priced his goods—the clubs were ten dollars, the TV twelve, the vacuum cleaner maybe thirteen, and the video game and the stroller nine each. He thought of making a sign saying BAR-GAINS, but he figured that people would stop anyway. And one did almost immediately, a Dodge Dart slowing to check things out. A black woman craned her head from the window and shouted, "What do you got?"

"Good stuff," he answered. "Golf clubs. You need a vacuum cleaner?"

The woman idled in the middle of the street, then revved the engine and drove off.

"Forget you, too!" he growled.

Mario sat on the front lawn for an hour, the shade slowly creeping away, taking with it the coolness of morning. A few cars passed, and so did people in the street. Every time they looked to consider the sale items from a distance, he stood up, hopeful. But they passed, unimpressed.

Mario began to get hot. He got himself a drink of water from the hose. He splashed his face with water and then noticed a lawn sprinkler sitting in a bed of mint. He unscrewed it from the hose and added it to his yard sale, thinking that his grandmother would never miss it.

Soon a car stopped and out came two women, both of them mothers, one heavy as a wheelbarrow and the other thin as a rake. Their babies stayed in the car, their hands pressed like starfish on the greasy windows. Both babies were working their teeth around pacifiers.

The women looked at the items, almost snickering, their mouths rolling in lassos of disgust.

"This is all you got?" the round mother asked.

"Most of it sold," Mario answered. "You should have been here earlier."

The women chuckled at his comment.

"How much for the TV?" the round mother asked.

Mario forgot. He gazed down at the TV, then bent down and turned the channel switch. His finger ran across the screen, gathering a clot of dust. "Sixteen dollars."

"For that?" she responded.

"It belonged to my uncle," Mario said. "He paid two hundred dollars for it."

"Yeah, sure," the skinny mother said.

"I'm selling it for him," Mario said. "He's dying of cancer."

The words didn't reach the women. They turned to leave, but the skinny mother spotted the sprinkler.

"Don't tell me this is sixteen dollars, too?" the skinny mother said.

"No," Mario answered, the sprinkler sparkling like a sword. "It's three dollars."

The mothers fell silent. Finally the skinny mother bargained. "I'll give you two."

Mario thought for a moment, let his teeth bite the insides of his cheeks. It wasn't really his, so it was no sweat off his back.

"OK," he said. "My uncle will appreciate it."

"What?" the round mother asked.

"He has cancer," Mario said. He told them that he was going to send the money right away because every bit helped.

The women paid for the sprinkler and left, their car pulling away with the unblinking eyes of the babies locked on him.

Minutes later a car pulled over and out stepped a man, a tattoo of a barking dog on each hard shoulder. His hair was slicked back. Both ears winked earrings in the shape of anchors.

"What's going on, champ?" the man asked. He stepped toward Mario but stopped in the shade. He was wearing cowboy boots, which were as small as a pig's trotters. He was lean. His tank top was white and didn't sport any emblems.

"Yard sale," Mario said. He waved to the house behind him and said, "My grandmother has cancer and needs to sell these things."

The man looked at the house, then Mario.

"Business good?" he asked.

"Pretty good." He scanned his array of stolen items, which now appeared crummy. "The best stuff has already been sold."

The man glared at Mario and then spat out, "Let's make a trade."

Mario looked cautiously at him.

"I'm selling radios," he explained. "Good ones. The kind you put on your shoulder." He told Mario that his brother-in-law had stolen them from his job but didn't have much use for them because he was sick.

"What's he got?" Mario asked. He moved closer to the man.

"Cancer," the man said. "It's going around."

Mario turned his face away and glanced at his grandmother's front curtain, which was still closed. He wondered if she was watching TV or just sitting staring at the wall.

"Listen, you're a smart-looking little dude. You should know a deal when you see one."

Mario studied the man, whose face now appeared as narrow as a hatchet.

"Where are they?" Mario asked. "What kind you got?"

"All brand names," the man responded, hooking a thumb in the direction of his car. "The best, little dude."

The two of them looked at each other, the man cool in the shade and Mario bubbling in his sweat. The man then turned and started toward his car. He brought out a large boom box, one with a CD changer and enough dials to confuse a genius.

"I'm telling you, little dude," the man crowed. "It's the best, and if you pass it up you'll be hating life." He placed the box on Mario's shoulders and flicked a switch.

The rap music thumped and vibrated against Mario's shoulders.

"What do you think?" the man asked after he took

away the boom box and turned off the music. "Forty dollars and..." He scanned the items on the lawn. "Some of these things."

Forty dollars, Mario thought. He had the twenty-five from the wedding, plus the two dollars from the sale of his grandmother's sprinkler.

"I don't have that much," Mario said.

"This is fine equipment," the man said. "What do you got then?"

"Twenty," Mario said, pushing a hand into his pocket. "Maybe a little bit more." He fingered the crumpled five.

The man told Mario that he should ask his grandmother, arguing that she would be happy if her grandson had his own boom box.

"I can't," he said. "She's sick, too."

"OK," the man mumbled, stomping one of his heels against the grass. "Let's do the trade."

The man took the TV, the video game, the clubs, the vacuum cleaner, but not before he got Mario's twenty and five. He placed the goods in the backseat of the car. He handed the boom box to Mario and then took it away.

"Hey, let me get you one in a box," he said. "You should have a clean one since you're such a good kid."

They walked to the car. The man opened up the trunk, where neat rows of boom boxes in cartons made Mario's eyes wide. He'd never seen such treasure.

"Go ahead. Take one," the man commanded.

Mario picked one on top and weighed it in his arms.

"It's solid!" the man sang. He slammed the trunk closed. "Sony makes the best."

Mario carried it to the patch of shade under the tree. Scraping with his fingernails, he opened the box and struggled to pull the boom box out of the Styrofoam casing. He thought of Christmas, how he would rip open presents in seconds and then cry because there was nothing else left to open. He ripped into the box and the plastic that surrounded the boom box.

"You need some batteries," the man informed Mario. "I got some, but they'll cost you."

Mario thought for a moment. He could ask his grandmother or hand over the money he got for the sprinkler.

"OK, except all I got is two bucks," Mario said.

The man almost skipped to his car and pulled open the glove compartment, bringing out four batteries.

"They're still good?" Mario asked, taking the batteries.

"These are the best," the man said simply. He snatched the two dollars from Mario. "You ever watch the commercial with the rabbit? These are those kind."

Mario didn't listen. He was already pushing off the back panel and sliding the batteries in.

"You have fun, little dude," the man said as he walked away, boots clicking, toward the car.

Mario fit in the last battery and closed the panel with a snap. He flicked on the switch, pushed dials, worked the volume and the stations, and raised the antenna. He shook the boom box. No music broke the silence of the quiet street.

"This one don't work!" he hollered to the car as it pulled away.

He played with more dials, then took off the back panel and fiddled with the batteries, thinking that perhaps he had put them in wrong. Then he felt a powdery red dust, which coated his fingertips. He rattled the boom box, and more dust rained. He took off the entire back of the boom box, and there in its guts were broken bricks.

He looked up at the place where the man had stood grinning. He felt weak, his shoulder blades like fallen wings. He lowered his eyes and with great fury punched the face of the boom box. Pain bit his knuckles and drew blood. He looked at his grandmother's front window, still curtained, and then he looked at the stroller.

That's where I belong, he thought. He felt like a baby on the lawn, some stupid tyke in diapers, a little brat whining for a broken toy. An infant in the art of scamming.

IF THE SHOE FITS

Manuel had four brothers and one sister, and when you counted his parents and the drift of uncles from Mexico, seasonal workers, his home was like a ship of pirates, all of them loud. His family played baseball in the living room, using the couch as first base, the recliner as second, and the floor furnace—a bad idea in winter when their sockless feet got burned—as third. Home plate was two old shirts stitched together and soaked with starch to make them hard. Because someone was always strumming a guitar or cooking at the stove or getting ready to bust the house with fun, Manuel didn't mind his raucous home.

What Manuel minded were the hand-me-down clothes he had to wear. His oldest brother was Hector, who passed his shirts and pants down to

Lalo, who passed them down to Samuel, who usually passed them into the garbage can. By then the clothes were almost shredded, the buttons missing or cracked, the fabric colorless, and the knees had holes large enough to push a head through.

Manuel got his hand-me-downs from Carlos, the brother directly above him in the hand-me-down chain. The clothes were usually in good shape but they fit awkwardly because Carlos was bigger than he was, huge in fact. While Manuel's oldest brothers were string beans, Carlos was big, not fat, and as strong and square as a box. So when Manuel slipped into the clothes Carlos had outgrown, the pants puddled around his ankles and the sleeves of the shirts hid his hands.

"Mom, I want my own clothes!" he cried one day when he put on Carlos's old jacket and it hung down to his knees.

"*Mi'jo,* it costs a lot of money," his mother tried to reason. She took the jacket off her son and shortened the sleeves and made the waistband tighter. Still, it hung oddly on his body.

"But Teresa gets new clothes," Manuel whined unhappily.

"That's because she's the only girl."

That was always her argument. Their sister, Teresa, the princess with the new this and new that, even got her own bedroom with a canopy bed, while the boys—all five—had to share one bedroom. At night they shared three beds, all of them snoring, coughing, talking in their sleep, and gnashing teeth until the sun rose and they got up to put on their hand-me-down clothes.

For Manuel's thirteenth birthday, his mom bought him a pair of new shoes, which he liked but didn't have much occasion to wear. He usually flopped about in tennis shoes, the laces undone. The new shoes were called loafers, but they were the fanciest shoes Manuel had ever owned because they had no laces to drag in the dirt. Manuel laughed when Teresa told him to put a penny in the front slot on top of each shoe. "That's the style," Teresa had told him, and to prove it searched through two magazines until she found a pair of shoes like his sporting pennies.

Then Manuel got a bigger idea. Instead of worthless pennies, he pushed in nickels, treating his shoes like parking meters. The effort it took to jam the nickels into the stiff leather nearly took his breath away.

"There," he said, exhausted. He slipped into his new shoes and clicked the heels together like Dorothy in *The Wizard of Oz*.

He walked around the house, dressed in a hand-me-down but spotless white shirt and a pair of pants whose crotch hung so low that he had to bend over to work the zipper. He paraded in front of the mirror and felt *suave*.

"Bond," he said to the face in the mirror. "James Bond."

He stared seriously as long as he could and then laughed like a clown.

Manuel decided to take his good looks outside to the playground. He marched down the street feeling stylish. He grinned at his new shoes and walked looking down, watching the nickels glinting in the sunlight. He picked up a stick from the curb and swung it like a cane. He stopped before a puddle of water on the sidewalk. To the reflection, he whispered, "Bond, James Bond—007."

Some little kids were on the swings and merry-go-round, and others were cracking stolen pomegranates on the edge of a table, something he did when he was their age. He would have joined them, but he was wearing his new shoes. He didn't want to risk staining them with the blood-red juice.

Manuel jingled coins in his pocket. He decided to splurge and buy himself a Mountain Dew soda. But as he rounded the corner to the soda machine, he stopped in his tracks. Angel Lara, the biggest *vato* of all *vatitos,* was there. Angel had his arm halfway up the chute of the machine and was trying to pull out a free soda. When Manuel turned to sneak away, Angel told him to stay right there if he cared about his life.

"How come you dressed like that, homes?" Angel

asked as he got up from his knees. His throat was dark with two tattoos—one was a cross and another a black spider with a red dot on its belly.

"I'm getting ready to go...," Manuel stammered, "...to a funeral."

"Who died?"

"My...aunt," Manuel lied. "She ate some bad hamburger meat."

"Before you put her in her grave, you liar, give me some money," Angel demanded. He extended his hand, tattooed with another black widow and a cross near his thumb.

"I don't got no money, man," Manuel lied a second time. His eyes were rolling in their sockets, a dead giveaway.

"You lie about this dead aunt, and now you lie about money," said Angel as he circled Manuel, who stood, head down, picking up the scent of Chee·tos on Angel's breath. "You want to keep your life *o qué?*"

"No, I'm not lying, Angel. I'm going to a funeral."

"You'll be the funeral if you don't cough up."

"I'm going to tell my brothers," Manuel threatened almost under his breath.

"Your brothers ain't nothing," Angel sneered. "I'll get my brothers to open a can of 'whip ass' if they try to do anything to me!"

Manuel knew that Angel's brothers were nasty as snakes, so he gave in. He coughed up the fifty-five cents in his pockets.

"And gimme those nickels, too," Angel demanded.

"Come on, Angel," Manuel pleaded.

"Come on, Angel," Angel mimicked.

Manuel took off his shoes and yanked and squeezed the nickels from the front of them.

Angel flipped a nickel into the air and slapped it against his palm. "Heads or tails."

Manuel, his mouth pulled down in sadness, muttered, "Tails."

Angel looked at the coin, then Manuel. "Guess again!"

"Heads."

"Sorry, homes! It was tails."

Angel laughed, the air about them stinking of Chee·tos. He fed the coins into the soda machine, and after a moment of indecision, he punched Mountain Dew, the same soda that Manuel would have chosen. Manuel licked his lips as Angel chugged on the soda, his Adam's apple bobbing up and down with each swallow.

Manuel went home and threw his shoes into the closet. He sulked for two weeks, but after two more weeks he forgot about Angel, who had gone to juvie for stealing a motorized wheelchair at the Fresno Fair.

Manuel kicked around in his tennies, which were dark with grass stains, blotted with motor oil, and bursting with holes where his big toes poked through, as large as sausages.

That month, he had a sudden growing spurt—a full inch in height and a thicker chest. Carlos's clothes began to hang better on his body. He felt strong. He felt that he could lift both his parents at the same time—Dad in his left arm and Mom (who was actually heavier) in his right arm.

"Mess with me, Angel, and you mess with life," shirtless Manuel whispered in front of the mirror. He whispered to make sure there was no chance that Angel might actually hear him. He made a muscle in his right arm and rubbed its oily shine.

Manuel's mom bought him a new pair of tennies, which she picked up at Kmart during a blue-light special. When she asked, "How come you don't wear your good shoes?" he answered that he was saving them for a special occasion.

The occasion arrived. He received an invitation in the mail to Kristi Hernandez's birthday party. Kristi's mother was a doctor, and her father was a manager for something or other, making her probably the richest kid at school. Not only that, she was good-looking and rumored to have written Manuel's name on her binder.

On the day of the party, he got dressed, splashing his face and throat with three different kinds of cologne. He brushed his teeth until they hurt and combed his hair four different ways. He settled on slicking his hair back.

"Bond," Manuel said to the mirror. "James Bond."

Then he brought out his fancy shoes from the closet, juggling them in the air and singing, "Kristi loves me, she loves me not! The homegirl better love me, or forget her!"

Then he tried to put the shoes on.

"Come on," he grunted. His face reddened, and his toes hurt. "Stupid shoes!"

After he got his feet into the shoes with tugs and groans, he stood up, wincing. He took a step. Pain stabbed the top part of his feet. He sat back down on the edge of his bed, not sure what to do. He couldn't wear his tennis shoes; even the new ones now looked old. He took off the loafers and pulled and yanked on the leather, hoping that they would loosen up. He beat them against the floor until his mother called from the kitchen for him to knock it off. He put on a pair of thinner socks even though they had holes in the heels.

"That's better," he said when he managed to squeeze his feet in. He took a step, and although they felt uncomfortable, they didn't hurt so much.

He left the house walking stiffly, with his poorly wrapped present, a Juan Gabriel CD that he had picked up from the dollar bin at Kmart.

He walked making a face, making *jeta* as his mother would say. His feet hurt, and each step was a stab of pain. He thought of returning home and asking his mother for a ride to Kristi's house, which was three miles away in the better part of town. But he knew that she would say that she was busy in the kitchen. She was expecting another uncle from Mexico.

He sat on someone's front lawn and took off the shoes.

"That feels good," he said as he wiggled each of his toes, beginning with the little piggy. He sighed and then stretched the shoes. He beat them against the lawn. But he put them back on in a flash when the owner of the house came out and not so nicely asked him to get out of his yard.

"I'm going, sir," he said, and left walking stiffly.

After a while he discovered that if he walked backward, his feet didn't hurt so much.

"I like this," he said to himself. There was almost no pain and, actually, another pleasure: He liked the view of where he had been better than the view of where he was going. The sky appeared bluer, the trees taller, the birds in the trees sweeter with song. He passed a woman raking leaves, and he said, "Hello." He didn't bother to explain.

He walked backward for nearly a mile and would have walked all the way to Kristi's house, except someone poked him in the back.

"How come you walking like a fool?" the voice demanded.

When he turned around, he discovered that the voice belonged to Angel.

"Angel!" Manuel's eyes grew as large as softballs.

"Don't yell, homes. I'm right here, not across the street." Angel sniffed the air and asked, "How come you stink?"

"It's cologne, not stink," Manuel corrected.

"Where you going dressed like that?"

Manuel started to explain, but Angel cut him off.

"Yeah, I know. One of your aunts grubbed on some bad meat, and you got to put her in the grave!" Angel laughed and ripped the Juan Gabriel CD from Manuel's hands. Before Manuel could stop him, Angel tore off the wrapping and, holding it in both hands, remarked, "That dude ain't nowhere. He's a chump!"

Manuel felt like crying. It was not only his feet; now even his present to Kristi was messed up.

"Here," Angel said, pushing the CD back into Manuel's clutches. "How come you're walking backward?"

Manuel bit his lower lip, not wanting to say.

"You got any money?"

Manuel brought out seventy-five cents from his pocket. He didn't want to argue with Angel.

"How about your shoes? You keep some coins there, *qué no?*"

Manuel shook his head. Tears hung like crystal chandeliers from his eyelashes.

"How come you're crying, punk! Did I hit you?"

He raised a hand as if to strike Manuel, who cowered and whined, "Come on, Angel. Leave me alone."

Manuel brushed away the tears.

"Take off your shoes and let me look."

Manuel did as he was told. Angel shoved his fists into the shoes and groped about. Finding nothing, he asked, "How come you like these girl shoes?"

"My mom bought them."

Angel sneered and let the shoes drop to the sidewalk. He left flipping one of Manuel's quarters.

Manuel sat on the lawn, depressed. He looked at the Juan Gabriel CD and the crumpled wrapping paper. He decided not to go to Kristi's party.

"When I grow up I'm gonna get him back," Manuel said of Angel. He slipped on his shoes and returned home, walking straight ahead as a punishment for being a wimp. I should have at least tried to hit the punk, he scolded himself. By the time he arrived home, his toes were throbbing like boom boxes, they hurt so badly.

In his room he listened to an oldies but goodies station, hoping for a song that would really make him sad. He would cry and let it all out, spilling a chandelier of tears. He pulled an old comic book from under his bed, one with an ad on how to beef up a body. He stared at the muscular guy in the ad: His stomach was like rocks and his arms like the boulders you find along rivers.

"I'm going to be like that," he promised himself. Right then he threw twenty-five punches and did forty-three push-ups. But he stopped when he spied a Three Musketeers bar sitting on the chest of drawers. He ate it greedily, promising himself that the next time it would be fruits and vegetables.

When his mother knocked on the door, he told her to go away. He began to blame his mother for his troubles. If she hadn't bought those shoes, Angel wouldn't have made me look so lame, he reasoned.

"Are you sick?" she asked, rapping on the door like a woodpecker.

"No," he answered, not bothering to explain.

But he came out for dinner when he smelled *enchiladas verdes*. He met his uncle Efrain from Mexico, the state of Sinaloa, a man as quiet as a saint. His uncle told them about the poverty of his town and how many of them had left in search of work in the United States.

"You're so lucky here," his uncle said. "You got food and clothes and a place to stay."

They watched this tiny man with a gray, wiry mustache. He ate with a lot of chewing, his mustache jumping about on his face. All five brothers and one sister, plus their mother and father, listened respectfully to this man, whose bronze-colored skin was as smooth as his wallet, which he brought out to show pictures of *his* family. He told stories about how as a boy he first worked selling Chiclets and sodas, then went on, as a young man, to sharpen scissors for a living. He told Manuel's family that he would be leaving the next day. He had a cousin in Merced who had promised him a job in a Chinese restaurant. He said that he had eaten Chinese food only twice, but with his new job he would have to get used to it.

After dinner the uncle said, "Let me help with the dishes."

"No, *hombre*," the father protested. "Leave them for the kids."

But the uncle joked that he had better get used to doing dishes. He wouldn't be talked out of it but did accept help from Manuel, the champ of greasy plates and forks. The two stood at the sink as it filled and the bubbles mounted. They got to work. While he pumped his arms up and down in the soapy water, Manuel noticed that his uncle's shoes were falling apart. His face lit up.

"*Tío*," Manuel said. "I got a present for you."

"*¿Qué?*" his uncle asked.

"It's a secret."

And it was a secret until the next morning, when Manuel woke early and placed his fancy leather shoes by the couch, where his uncle slept, mustache twitching even in sleep.

"*¿Qué es?*" his uncle asked. "What's this?"

Manuel told him that he needed some new shoes. His uncle rolled from the couch and took the shoes into his hands. He turned them over and over and said, "*Mi'jo,* what's your name?"

"Manuel."

The uncle patted Manuel's face and said, "That's a good name."

The uncle ate a light breakfast and left just as the other kids began to stir from bed. Manuel, standing in his socks on the front porch, wished this uncle good luck, *buena suerte,* in those shoes with slots for pennies brown as his work-darkened skin.

FRANKIE THE ROOSTER

José Luis, a seventh grader at Fort Miller Junior High, got a chance to play Cupid one Saturday morning, just after a hearty breakfast of *chorizo con huevos*. His chance came when the telephone rang.

He was watching Roller Derby with his father, a couch *papa* on the weekends. He jumped to his feet, yelling, "I got it!" and hurried to the hallway telephone.

"Hey," the voice said.

"Hey, yourself," José Luis answered. "Who's this?"

"Your *primo*—Ricardo."

Ricardo was José Luis's cousin. He was so good-looking that he had once modeled a shirt from Kmart in a newspaper ad. It had created a stir at school. The girls had flocked around him like sea-gulls on a bag of french fries.

"What's up?" José Luis asked.

"I can't tell you now," Ricardo said. "But if you want to earn a couple of bucks, get down to my house."

José Luis liked money, provided that he didn't have to sweat too much. He decided to go down to his cousin's place. He hauled off on his bike, doing a wheelie that lasted nearly a block. Two neighborhood dogs barked behind chain-link fences, and José Luis just shouted, "See ya!"

When he arrived, Ricardo was stretched out on the lawn sucking on a stalk of grass. He was wearing the shirt from the Kmart ad. José Luis skidded to a stop and hopped off his bike. He tossed it on the lawn and threw himself down next to Ricardo.

"What's wrong?" José Luis asked when he noticed Ricardo's gloomy face.

"Can I trust you?" Ricardo asked as he sat up.

José Luis nodded his head.

Ricardo pulled a letter from his shirt pocket and waved it at his cousin. The letter gave off a scent of cologne and the envelope read: "To Sylvia, My Eternal Flower."

"I want you to deliver this letter to Sylvia."

"Me?" José Luis asked, pointing at himself.

"Yeah." Ricardo pulled three dollars from his pocket and slapped them into José Luis's palms.

"But you're the Romeo," José Luis said. "Girls go crazy for you."

"I know, homes, I know," Ricardo said, sighing.

But he told his cousin that Sylvia's father had run him off with a spray from the garden hose.

"That's cold!" José Luis said sympathetically. He paused and risked asking what was in the letter.

"My thoughts," Ricardo answered. "Don't get nosy. You want the job or not?"

José Luis nodded his head. He got Sylvia's address and promised to deliver the letter, which he first sniffed and then slipped respectfully into his shirt pocket. After all, it was his cousin's heart in those words.

"I'll get it done, *primo,*" José Luis said, and jumped on his bike. He pedaled hard, so hard that his ears got cold and the letter in his pocket seemed to sing in the wind. He slowed down but soon picked up speed again because a dog with a long purple tongue began to chase him.

He lost the dog and pulled onto Sylvia's street. He rode on the sidewalk, hands stuffed in his pockets, and searched for the address.

It's 916 . . . or was it 918? he thought to himself, confused. He stopped in front of 916. The house was pink with scraggly rose bushes and a TV antenna flopped over on top of the roof. There were fancy Spanish-style bars over two windows.

"I think this is it," he said to himself as he straddled his bike and stared at the house. Somewhere in the back a dog began to bark and a city rooster crowed.

He climbed the steps, but before he could knock, a man came out and said in singsong Spanish, "May I help you?" The man was dressed like a cowboy, with a silver-plated belt buckle and cowboy boots. A turquoise ring gleamed on his gnarled hand.

"I'm looking for a girl."

"*¿Quién?*" the man asked. A web of fine lines showed up in the corners of his steel-colored eyes.

"Sylvia," José Luis said, slightly afraid of this old cowboy. From his shirt pocket, he pulled out the letter, the fumes of the cologne making him sneeze. He sneezed two more times before he could explain his presence.

The man sized up José Luis. Without taking his eyes off him, he called, "Sylvia, *ven acá. Hay un muchacho aquí.*"

A woman, not a girl, came out onto the porch. Her hair was a hive of uncombed curls. She was wearing a Raiders T-shirt and sipped from a Raiders coffee cup. "What does this handsome young man want?" she said playfully.

"I got a letter for Sylvia." But even as José Luis handed her the letter, he knew he was at the wrong address. He wanted to grab the letter back, but instead he played it cool. "Maybe it's for another Sylvia."

The woman put the coffee cup down on the porch railing and turned the letter over in her hand. Curious, she sniffed its cologne. She looked at the words *To Sylvia, My Eternal Flower.*

Her husband, José Luis noticed, seemed to puff up with anger as he looked over the woman's shoulder. His hands went up to his lean hips.

"I never get letters," Sylvia remarked as she ripped it open. She read it, her eyes bright with happiness. "Oh, it's so sweet." She slowly handed it back to José Luis. "But it's not for me, *muchacho.*" She pointed at the neighbor's house and said, "I think it's for the Sylvia *there.*"

He turned and looked into the neighboring yard. Laundry hung like colorful flags from the backyard.

"Yeah, I think I have the wrong address," José Luis agreed in a near whisper. He smiled at the man, then the woman, then the man again. He told them to have a nice day and apologized for bothering them. When he turned to leave, he was confronted by the rooster he'd heard when he first arrived. It crowed and strutted toward him.

"Frankie!" the woman scolded. "Go back to the backyard!"

The rooster was nearly as tall as the rosebush, and his hooklike feet looked just as thorny.

"Nice Frankie," José Luis cooed, clicking his fingers and trying to sound friendly.

When José Luis left the yard and started over to the real Sylvia's house, the rooster followed him. He tried to shoo it away, but the rooster just jumped back and fluttered his burnt-orange wings. José Luis stomped his feet, but the rooster was fearless.

"I'm going to make you into soup, chicken," José Luis scolded the rooster. "If you don't watch it, you're going to be a plate of chicken *enchiladas!*"

Frankie crowed and pecked at a candy wrapper on the sidewalk. Then he picked up a cigarette butt with his beak. Before he dropped it, the rooster looked like he was smoking.

"You jughead chicken," José Luis said, laughing. "You look like a gangster."

José Luis entered the neighbor's yard, set his bike on the lawn, and climbed the steps of the porch. The rooster followed along.

"Get out of here!" José Luis scolded.

The rooster blinked its eyes and crowed.

"Shut up, man!" José Luis demanded angrily just as the front door opened. He turned to face a girl who was about sixteen. Her eyes were dark with mascara, and a tattoo twisted around her wrist like a snake.

"Not you," he apologized. "Him! Frankie." He stabbed a finger at the rooster, who crowed again, this time louder, and made a noisy fan of its wings.

Sylvia looked down at the rooster. "I thought they cooked him last week."

"They're going to cook Frankie?" José Luis cried. For a second he pictured Frankie in a pot boiling on the back burner.

"That's what I heard."

The two of them stared silently at the rooster, and the rooster stared at them. José Luis was sorry for his wisecrack about chicken *enchiladas.*

Sylvia broke the silence. "What do you want?"

"Ricardo told me to give this to you."

Sylvia smiled as she took the letter.

"It's none of my business, but he likes you a lot." A red glow blossomed on José Luis's face. "He says—"

Sylvia's father stepped out onto the porch. He gazed at his daughter and then the boy, sizing up the meaning of their gathering. His face was stern and creased with deep lines. "What do you want, *muchacho*?" her father asked gruffly.

"Nothing really," José Luis said, with a shrug. "I was dropping off something for Sylvia."

The father's attention turned to the rooster. "I thought they cooked Frankie last week." He ran a large work-toughened hand around his chin.

Again, José Luis felt bad for the rooster. He was more than sorry for cracking jokes about Frankie. Right then he decided to cut out chicken from his diet.

"Well, I gotta go," José Luis said. He turned and

bounced down the stairs. He picked up his bike, waved *adiós* to Sylvia and her father, and left the yard, glad that his mission was accomplished. Frankie followed.

"Go away, man," José Luis yelled. *"¡Ándale!"*

Frankie blinked his eyes at him and crowed.

José Luis straddled his bike and pushed off. To his surprise, Frankie fluttered after him. The rooster was fast, but not fast enough to keep up. José Luis looked back.

"Poor Frankie," he muttered to himself.

He recalled his visit to his grandparents in Arizona and how they had wrung the necks of two chickens that had cried the *grito* of death, fluttering their feathery bodies for two full minutes. Later, through his tears and shoulder-jerking sobs, José Luis was forced to eat them with a large soup spoon.

José Luis skidded to a stop and turned back. He bought Frankie with the three dollars Ricardo had given him. The cowboy-looking man helped fit Frankie into a red potato sack. Then José Luis pushed off, with one hand on the handlebars and the other hand pressing a city rooster to his chest.

That was how José Luis got his pet rooster, and how Frankie started problems for his family. His father liked the rooster, which reminded him of his days growing up in Arizona. He told his family over dinner how he would milk cows, pitch hay, gather eggs, and, swallowing, chop off the heads of chickens.

"*Pues,* it was good back then," he said fondly, patting his stomach that was now round as a globe. "Every boy needs his own rooster."

But his mother had other feelings about Frankie. On the second day after Frankie's arrival, she had discovered that he had pecked all the leaves off her geraniums. The plants were now mere sticks in coffee cans.

"I'm going to get him," his mother vowed, and chased Frankie until she was out of breath.

On the third day, he got into the house and tipped over plants, ashtrays, and family portraits. Nastier than a cat, he clawed the curtains on the front window. He left droppings on a new throw rug in the hallway.

"That bird is going into the pot!" his mom cried while opening a can of chicken gumbo soup.

But Frankie's most grievous error was going into Señor Garcia's yard. *El señor* was blind and spent most of his time whittling religious crosses while sitting under his mulberry tree. Frankie jumped the fence, fluttering down like a tossed telephone book. He had the audacity to peck Señor Garcia, whose arm, a day later, became infected with blood poisoning. It grew huge as a porpoise.

"*¡Travieso!* A troublemaker!" José Luis's mother cried. "He's got to go!"

They paid for Señor Garcia's doctor bills, which added up to thirty-five dollars, a reasonable sum because Señor Garcia was a decent man and he took some of the blame because he had beckoned the chicken. He, too, grew up on a farm and enjoyed animals.

Frankie spooked children on the block and stopped cars when he wandered into the street looking for cigarette butts or other interesting things. He was often seen strutting around with a cigarette dangling from his mouth. Perhaps it was this taste for strange things that made him ill. One day José Luis went outside and discovered Frankie with his clawed feet jutting straight up in the air.

"What's wrong!" José Luis cried. He dropped to his knees and felt the rooster's breast. Behind the layers of feathers, he located a thump of a heartbeat. The rooster let out a feeble crow.

José Luis picked up his pet and showed his father, who was leaving for work.

"He's sick, *papi*," José Luis cried, raising Frankie up like an offering to a pagan god.

Sighing, his father examined the chicken and concluded that Frankie must have eaten something bad. He suggested that they keep him in the garage and let his stomach rest for a day.

José Luis went off to school, and after the last bell rang, he biked home, laying a twenty-foot skid on the cement patio in the backyard. He tossed his bike aside and called out, "Frankie! Jughead!" He pulled open the door to the garage, where he had left the rooster sitting in a cardboard box. Frankie wasn't there.

José Luis went inside. His mother was at the stove stirring a pot with a wooden spoon. He tiptoed behind his mother and gave her a hug. He looked into the pot. On the surface floated carrots and celery. Then he saw a chicken wing jut up from the broth and sink to the bottom. He swallowed. Mom killed Frankie, he thought. He saw the wing jut up again as his mother stirred, this time adding three shakes of salt. Then he noticed other parts—breast and drumstick, all dismembered like in some grisly horror movie.

"Mom?" José Luis asked, trying not to let her see the sadness welling up in a large knot in his throat.

"Yes?" she asked as she moved from the stove to the kitchen counter. She gathered up a handful of chopped onions in her cupped hands and hurried quickly to the stove. She tossed them into the pot and wiped her hands on her apron.

"That's not Frankie, is it?" he asked. He jerked his chin at the pot.

"Frankie? That scraggly thing?" She stood with her hands on her hips, the stirring spoon dripping three drips to the floor. "You think I'd bother to chop his head off and put him in one of *my* pots?"

"Don't play with me, Mom," José Luis whined.

A pearl-shaped tear ran from the corner of her left eye.

"You're crying because you killed Frankie, huh?" he continued. "How could you, Mom? He's our pet!"

"You crazy kid," she said. She wiped her eyes and laughed. "It's the onions, not Frankie." She told him that Frankie was outside. She had let him out of the garage because he had pecked a hole in a bag of rice in their food pantry.

Frankie was on the side of the house. The rooster looked better than in the morning, but he still seemed sick. José Luis sat down with the rooster and petted his feathers and cooed for him to get better.

The next morning, Saturday, Frankie was on his back again, his thorny legs in the air. He squawked when José Luis petted his feathers. His eyes looked watery.

"We got to take him to the vet!" José Luis begged.

His parents stood solemnly over the rooster. José Luis's father nudged Frankie with his boot, not wanting to touch him.

"*Mi'jo,* we can't spend money like that," his mother said.

José Luis begged his parents, promising to be a good kid forever and ever.

His parents were unmoved.

"I'll, I'll . . . ," José Luis stuttered. "I'll rip out all

those weeds." He pointed to weeds that stood as tall as spears where the summer before they had kept a garden.

His parents looked at each other, each raising an eyebrow, suddenly interested.

"OK, it's a deal," his father said, but he added, "and the flower bed up front."

All four gathered in the car and drove down to the Olive Street Veterinarian, where one door was marked CATS and the other DOGS. José Luis rushed into the CAT door, figuring that if Frankie got into a fight, he could hold his own against an alley cat. A dog was a different matter.

After signing some forms, he was told to take his rooster into the examination room. The vet soon came in. Right away José Luis felt hopeful because the man had a little wattle of skin jiggling under his chin. His head was bald, and his eyes were as small as a chicken's.

"So what's wrong with...," the vet asked, looking down at his clipboard, "...with Frankie?"

"I don't know," José Luis said. "He ain't doing nothing. He's just lying around."

The vet took Frankie's head into his hands and felt his throat, squeezing it until Frankie squawked.

"His air passage is clear," the vet remarked. He next felt his breast and then took a quick peek at Frankie's rump. He listened to his heart and shone a light in his eyes. "If you don't mind," the vet said after he lifted a fan of wing and let it spread, "I would like to keep him for a day or two."

José Luis thought about the money that would be forked over. It would anger his father, but he had said that every boy needs a rooster. He petted Frankie and said, "Don't worry, man. I'll take care of you. I won't let you down." To the vet, he said, "OK."

He went to confront his parents in the waiting room. His father was petting a cat, smiling, his face bright with happiness. It was a perfect time.

"*Papi,* they're going to keep Frankie for a day," he said with a lilt to his voice. "They need to observe him."

"Observe him!" his father stood up, pushing the cat aside. "I'll observe him in a chicken *enchilada!*"

"Dad, it's Frankie, our pet. He loves you!"

"It's going to cost money!" his mother argued.

"I'll work for Frankie, Mom." He told his mom that he would paint the garage like she wanted.

"Chickens are for the farm, not the city!" his father snapped.

"But, Dad, you said every boy needs a rooster. That's what you said!" José Luis surprised himself. He never argued with his father, but this was a matter of life or death. At least for Frankie.

They left Frankie there, and when they returned two days later, the bill came to $97.35.

"You keep him!" the father yelled in Spanish, the

language he turned to when he was really upset. "Deep fry him, *no importa.* Use his feathers for a pillow, *no importa.*"

Just beyond the reception desk, Frankie was crowing behind the bars of a cage.

"Come on, Dad! I'll do anything! Frankie loves us!"

Frankie crowed as if in agreement.

His father, purple with rage, paid the bill. They released Frankie with a bottle of pills that the receptionist said José Luis should stuff down Frankie's throat three times a day.

"If he gets worse, just give us a call," she said with a chime in her voice. "He's a really cute chicken."

"Rooster," José Luis corrected.

His father muttered in Spanish all the way home and warned his son not to tell anyone, including his mother, that he had spent that kind of money saving a chicken. By the time they pulled into the driveway, José Luis's father was laughing hysterically, laughing and crying that he was the dumbest man on the planet.

"A hundred dollars for a chicken! *¡Tontos!*"

José Luis assured him that he wasn't dumb but caring. He told his father that he was a great humanitarian, a fancy word he had learned a few weeks before in history class.

Frankie jumped from the car window, spread his wings, and strutted on the lawn. Although it was already almost noon, he let out a crow that echoed through the street and sent up a swarm of sparrows from a tree. He crowed and Señor Garcia, with his granddaughter leading his walk, said in Spanish, "*Ay, el gallo ha vuelto!* The rooster has returned."

He returned, but a week later he disappeared from the yard, leaving only a few burnished feathers on the back porch. Everyone concluded that he must have gotten tugged away by a dog.

"I'm a *tonto!*" José Luis's father cried. "I spent all this money on a chicken and the stupid thing goes away."

His mother appeared relieved and that afternoon began to replant her yard with flowers. But she was sad for her son, who cried in the garage all by himself, cried that no one loved him or his rooster. Later José Luis set the only photo of Frankie— a snapshot of Frankie on the garage roof—before a homemade altar of candles and a few remaining feathers. And when his good-looking cousin, Ricardo, called and asked him to deliver another letter, this time a girl named Francisca, José Luis hung up. But not before telling his cousin that he was a source of a lot of his pain.

In Frankie's honor, José Luis's mom didn't serve chicken to her family for a month. But when she did, chicken tacos, everyone ate in silence.

"You know, Mom," José Luis said halfway through dinner. He wiped his mouth and began to sprinkle *salsa* on his third taco. "I think Frankie would have tasted pretty good."

"If we'd cooked him?" she asked, her face close to the plate.

"Yeah, like these . . . tacos," he said. He started to bite into the taco but stopped, wondering if Frankie really disappeared or if his mother was behind it all. Maybe she had chopped off his head or choked him behind the garage and then tossed him into the freezer. He looked at the taco in his hands and then at his mother, who was raising her own taco—her third, he noticed—into her mouth.

"Yeah, with your cooking," José Luis said wisely, "Frankie would have tasted really good." He watched his mother bite into her taco, the shell cracking like bone and the tomato running like blood on her fingers.

BORN WORKER

They said that José was born with a ring of dirt around his neck, with grime under his fingernails, and skin calloused from the grainy twist of a shovel. They said his palms were already rough by the time he was three, and soon after he learned his primary colors, his squint was the squint of an aged laborer. They said he was a born worker. By seven he was drinking coffee slowly, his mouth pursed the way his mother sipped. He wore jeans, a shirt with sleeves rolled to his elbows. His eye could measure a length of board, and his knees genuflected over flower beds and leafy gutters.

They said lots of things about José, but almost nothing of his parents. His mother stitched at a machine all day, and his father, with a steady job at the telephone company, climbed splintered, sun-sucked poles, fixed wires and looked around the city at tree level.

"What do you see up there?" José once asked his father.

"Work," he answered. "I see years of work, *mi'jo.*"

José took this as a truth, and though he did well in school, he felt destined to labor. His arms would pump, his legs would bend, his arms would carry a world of earth. He believed in hard work, believed that his strength was as ancient as a rock's.

"Life is hard," his father repeated from the time José could first make out the meaning of words until he was stroking his fingers against the grain of his sandpaper beard.

His mother was an example to José. She would raise her hands, showing her fingers pierced from the sewing machines. She bled on her machine, bled because there was money to make, a child to raise, and a roof to stay under.

One day when José returned home from junior high, his cousin Arnie was sitting on the lawn sucking on a stalk of grass. José knew that grass didn't come from his lawn. His was cut and pampered, clean.

"José!" Arnie shouted as he took off the earphones of his CD Walkman.

"Hi, Arnie," José said without much enthusiasm.

He didn't like his cousin. He thought he was lazy and, worse, spoiled by the trappings of being middle class. His parents had good jobs in offices and showered him with clothes, shoes, CDs, vacations, almost anything he wanted. Arnie's family had never climbed a telephone pole to size up the future.

Arnie rose to his feet, and José saw that his cousin was wearing a new pair of high-tops. He didn't say anything.

"Got an idea," Arnie said cheerfully. "Something that'll make us money."

José looked at his cousin, not a muscle of curiosity twitching in his face.

Still, Arnie explained that since he himself was so clever with words, and his best cousin in the whole world was good at working with his hands, that maybe they might start a company.

"What would you do?" José asked.

"Me?" he said brightly. "Shoot, I'll round up all kinds of jobs for you. You won't have to do anything." He stopped, then started again. "Except— you know—do the work."

"Get out of here," José said.

"Don't be that way," Arnie begged. "Let me tell you how it works."

The boys went inside the house, and while José stripped off his school clothes and put on his jeans and a T-shirt, Arnie told him that they could be rich.

"You ever hear of this guy named Bechtel?" Arnie asked.

José shook his head.

"Man, he started just like us," Arnie said. "He started digging ditches and stuff, and the next thing you knew, he was sitting by his own swimming pool. You want to sit by your own pool, don't you?" Arnie smiled, waiting for José to speak up.

"Never heard of this guy Bechtel," José said after he rolled on two huge socks, worn at the heels. He opened up his chest of drawers and brought out a packet of Kleenex.

Arnie looked at the Kleenex.

"How come you don't use your sleeve?" Arnie joked.

José thought for a moment and said, "I'm not like you." He smiled at his retort.

"Listen, I'll find the work, and then we can split it fifty-fifty."

José knew fifty-fifty was a bad deal.

"How about sixty-forty?" Arnie suggested when he could see that José wasn't going for it. "I know a lot of people from my dad's job. They're waiting for us."

José sat on the edge of his bed and started to lace up his boots. He knew that there were agencies that would find you work, agencies that took a portion of your pay. They're cheats, he thought, people who sit in air-conditioned offices while others work.

"You really know a lot of people?" José asked.

"Boatloads," Arnie said. "My dad works with this millionaire—honest—who cooks a steak for his dog every day."

He's a liar, José thought. No matter how he tried, he couldn't picture a dog grubbing on steak. The world was too poor for that kind of silliness.

"Listen, I'll go eighty-twenty," José said.

"Aw, man," Arnie whined. "That ain't fair."

José laughed.

"I mean, half the work is finding the jobs," Arnie explained, his palms up as he begged José to be reasonable.

José knew this was true. He had had to go door-to-door, and he disliked asking for work. He assumed that it should automatically be his since he was a good worker, honest, and always on time.

"Where did you get this idea, anyhow?" José asked.

"I got a business mind," Arnie said proudly.

"Just like that Bechtel guy," José retorted.

"That's right."

José agreed to a seventy-thirty split, with the condition that Arnie had to help out. Arnie hollered, arguing that some people were meant to work and others to come up with brilliant ideas. He was one of the latter. Still, he agreed after José said it was that or nothing.

In the next two weeks, Arnie found an array of jobs. José peeled off shingles from a rickety garage roof, carried rocks down a path to where a pond would go, and spray-painted lawn furniture. And while Arnie accompanied him, most of the time he did nothing. He did help occasionally. He did shake the cans of spray paint and kick aside debris so that José didn't trip while going down the path carrying the rocks. He did stack the piles of shingles, but almost cried when a nail bit his thumb. But mostly he told José what he had missed or where the work could be improved. José was bothered because he and his work had never been criticized before.

But soon José learned to ignore his cousin, ignore his comments about his spray painting, or about the way he lugged rocks, two in each arm. He didn't say anything, either, when they got paid and Arnie rubbed his hands like a fly, muttering, "It's payday."

Then Arnie found a job scrubbing a drained swimming pool. The two boys met early at José's house. Arnie brought his bike. José's own bike had a flat that grinned like a clown's face.

"I'll pedal," José suggested when Arnie said that he didn't have much leg strength.

With Arnie on the handlebars, José tore off, his pedaling so strong that tears of fear formed in Arnie's eyes.

"Slow down!" Arnie cried.

José ignored him and within minutes they were riding the bike up a gravel driveway. Arnie hopped off at first chance.

"You're scary," Arnie said, picking a gnat from his eye.

José chuckled.

When Arnie knocked on the door, an old man still in pajamas appeared in the window. He motioned for the boys to come around to the back.

"Let me do the talking," Arnie suggested to his cousin. "He knows my dad real good. They're like this." He pressed two fingers together.

José didn't bother to say OK. He walked the bike into the backyard, which was lush with plants— roses in their last bloom, geraniums, hydrangeas, pansies with their skirts of bright colors. José could make out the splash of a fountain. Then he heard the hysterical yapping of a poodle. From all his noise, a person might have thought the dog was on fire.

"Hi, Mr. Clemens," Arnie said, extending his hand. "I'm Arnie Sanchez. It's nice to see you again."

José had never seen a kid actually greet someone like this. Mr. Clemens said, hiking up his pajama bottoms, "I only wanted one kid to work."

"Oh," Arnie stuttered. "Actually, my cousin José really does the work and I kind of, you know, supervise."

Mr. Clemens pinched up his wrinkled face. He

seemed not to understand. He took out a pea-sized hearing aid, fiddled with its tiny dial, and fit it into his ear, which was surrounded with wiry gray hair.

"I'm only paying for one boy," Mr. Clemens shouted. His poodle click-clicked and stood behind his legs. The dog bared its small crooked teeth.

"That's right," Arnie said, smiling a strained smile. "We know that you're going to compensate only one of us."

Mr. Clemens muttered under his breath. He combed his hair with his fingers. He showed José the pool, which was shaped as round as an elephant. It was filthy with grime. Near the bottom some grayish water shimmered and leaves floated as limp as cornflakes.

"It's got to be real clean," Mr. Clemens said, "or it's not worth it."

"Oh, José's a great worker," Arnie said. He patted his cousin's shoulders and said that he could lift a mule.

Mr. Clemens sized up José and squeezed his shoulders, too.

"How do I know you, anyhow?" Mr. Clemens asked Arnie, who was aiming a smile at the poodle.

"You know my dad," Arnie answered, raising his smile to the old man. "He works at Interstate Insurance. You and he had some business deals."

Mr. Clemens thought for a moment, a hand on his

mouth, head shaking. He could have been thinking about the meaning of life, his face was so dark.

"Mexican fella?" he inquired.

"That's him," Arnie said happily.

José felt like hitting his cousin for his cheerful attitude. Instead, he walked over and picked up the white plastic bottle of bleach. Next to it were a wire brush, a pumice stone, and some rags. He set down the bottle and, like a surgeon, put on a pair of rubber gloves.

"You know what you're doing, boy?" Mr. Clemens asked.

José nodded as he walked into the pool. If it had been filled with water, his chest would have been wet. The new hair on his chest would have been floating like the legs of a jellyfish.

"Oh yeah," Arnie chimed, speaking for his cousin. "José was born to work."

José would have drowned his cousin if there had been more water. Instead, he poured a bleach solution into a rag and swirled it over an area. He took the wire brush and scrubbed. The black algae came up like a foamy monster.

"We're a team," Arnie said to Mr. Clemens.

Arnie descended into the pool and took the bleach bottle from José. He held it for José and smiled up at Mr. Clemens, who, hands on hips, watched for a while, the poodle at his side. He cupped his ear, as if to pick up the sounds of José's scrubbing.

"Nice day, huh?" Arnie sang.

"What?" Mr. Clemens said.

"Nice day," Arnie repeated, this time louder. "So which ear can't you hear in?" Grinning, Arnie wiggled his ear to make sure that Mr. Clemens knew what he was asking.

Mr. Clemens ignored Arnie. He watched José, whose arms worked back and forth like he was sawing logs.

"We're not only a team," Arnie shouted, "but we're also cousins."

Mr. Clemens shook his head at Arnie. When he left, the poodle leading the way, Arnie immediately climbed out of the pool and sat on the edge, legs dangling.

"It's going to be blazing," Arnie complained. He shaded his eyes with his hand and looked east, where the sun was rising over a sycamore, its leaves hanging like bats.

José scrubbed. He worked the wire brush over the black and green stains, the grime dripping like tears. He finished a large area. He hopped out of the pool and returned hauling a garden hose with an attached nozzle. He gave the cleaned area a blast. When the spray got too close, his cousin screamed, got up, and, searching for something to do, picked a loquat from a tree.

"What's your favorite fruit?" Arnie asked.

José ignored him.

Arnie stuffed a bunch of loquats into his mouth, then cursed himself for splattering juice on his new high-tops. He returned to the pool, his cheeks fat with the seeds, and once again sat at the edge. He started to tell José how he had first learned to swim. "We were on vacation in Mazatlán. You been there, ain't you?"

José shook his head. He dabbed the bleach solution onto the sides of the pool with a rag and scrubbed a new area.

"Anyhow, my dad was on the beach and saw this drowned dead guy," Arnie continued. "And right there, my dad got scared and realized I couldn't swim."

Arnie rattled on about how his father had taught him in the hotel pool and later showed him where the drowned man's body had been.

"Be quiet," José said.

"What?"

"I can't concentrate," José said, stepping back to look at the cleaned area.

Arnie shut his mouth but opened it to lick loquat juice from his fingers. He kicked his legs against the swimming pool, bored. He looked around the backyard and spotted a lounge chair. He got up, dusting off the back of his pants, and threw himself into the cushions. He raised and lowered the back of the lounge. Sighing, he snuggled in. He stayed quiet for three minutes, during which time José scrubbed. His arms hurt but he kept working with long strokes. José knew that in an hour the sun would drench the pool with light. He hurried to get the job done.

Arnie then asked, "You ever peel before?"

José looked at his cousin. His nose burned from the bleach. He scrunched up his face.

"You know, like when you get sunburned."

"I'm too dark to peel," José said, his words echoing because he had advanced to the deep end. "Why don't you be quiet and let me work?"

Arnie babbled on that he had peeled when on vacation in Hawaii. He explained that he was really more French than Mexican, and that's why his skin was sensitive. He said that when he lived in France, people thought that he could be Portuguese or maybe Armenian, never Mexican.

José felt like soaking his rag with bleach and pressing it over Arnie's mouth to make him be quiet.

Then Mr. Clemens appeared. He was dressed in white pants and a flowery shirt. His thin hair was combed so that his scalp, as pink as a crab, showed.

"I'm just taking a little rest," Arnie said.

Arnie leaped back into the pool. He took the bleach bottle and held it. He smiled at Mr. Clemens, who came to inspect their progress.

"José's doing a good job," Arnie said, then whistled a song.

Mr. Clemens peered into the pool, hands on knees, admiring the progress.

"Pretty good, huh?" Arnie asked.

Mr. Clemens nodded. Then his hearing aid fell out, and José turned in time to see it roll like a bottle cap toward the bottom of the pool. It leaped into the stagnant water with a plop. A single bubble went up, and it was gone.

"Dang," Mr. Clemens swore. He took shuffling steps toward the deep end. He steadied his gaze on where the hearing aid had sunk. He leaned over and suddenly, arms waving, one leg kicking out, he tumbled into the pool. He landed standing up, then his legs buckled, and he crumbled, his head striking against the bottom. He rolled once, and half of his body settled in the water.

"Did you see that!" Arnie shouted, big-eyed.

José had already dropped his brushes on the side of the pool and hurried to the old man, who moaned, eyes closed, his false teeth jutting from his mouth. A ribbon of blood immediately began to flow from his scalp.

"We better get out of here!" Arnie suggested. "They're going to blame us!"

José knelt on both knees at the old man's side. He took the man's teeth from his mouth and placed them in his shirt pocket. The old man groaned and opened his eyes, which were shiny wet. He appeared startled, like a newborn.

"Sir, you'll be all right," José cooed, then snapped at his cousin. "Arnie, get over here and help me!"

"I'm going home," Arnie whined.

"You punk!" José yelled. "Go inside and call 911."

Arnie said that they should leave him there.

"Why should we get involved?" he cried as he started for his bike. "It's his own fault."

José laid the man's head down and with giant steps leaped out of the pool, shoving his cousin as he passed. He went into the kitchen and punched in 911 on a telephone. He explained to the operator what had happened. When asked the address, José dropped the phone and went onto the front porch to look for it.

"It's 940 East Brown," José breathed. He hung up and looked wildly about the kitchen. He opened up the refrigerator and brought out a plastic tray of ice, which he twisted so that a few of the cubes popped out and slid across the floor. He wrapped some cubes in a dish towel. When he raced outside, Arnie was gone, the yapping poodle was doing laps around the edge of the pool, and Mr. Clemens was trying to stand up.

"No, sir," José said as he jumped into the pool, his own knees almost buckling. "Please, sit down."

Mr. Clemens staggered and collapsed. José caught him before he hit his head again. The towel of ice cubes dropped from his hands. With his legs spread to absorb the weight, José raised the man up in his arms, this fragile man. He picked him up and carefully stepped toward the shallow end, one slow elephant step at a time.

"You'll be all right," José said, more to himself than to Mr. Clemens, who moaned and struggled to be let free.

The sirens wailed in the distance. The poodle yapped, which started a dog barking in the neighbor's yard.

"You'll be OK," José repeated, and in the shallow end of the pool, he edged up the steps. He lay the old man in the lounge chair and raced back inside for more ice and another towel. He returned outside and placed the bundle of cubes on the man's head, where the blood flowed. Mr. Clemens was awake, looking about. When the old man felt his mouth, José reached into his shirt pocket and pulled out his false teeth. He fit the teeth into Mr. Clemens's mouth and a smile appeared, something bright at a difficult time.

"I hit my head," Mr. Clemens said after smacking his teeth so that the fit was right.

José looked up and his gaze floated to a telephone pole, one his father might have climbed. If he had been there, his father would have seen that José was more than just a good worker. He would have seen a good man. He held the towel to the old man's head. The poodle, now quiet, joined them on the lounge chair.

A fire truck pulled into the driveway and soon

they were surrounded by firemen, one of whom brought out a first-aid kit. A fireman led José away and asked what had happened. He was starting to explain when his cousin reappeared, yapping like a poodle.

"I was scrubbing the pool," Arnie shouted, "and I said, 'Mr. Clemens, you shouldn't stand so close to the edge.' But did he listen? No, he leaned over and ... Well, you can just imagine my horror."

José walked away from Arnie's jabbering. He walked away, and realized that there were people like his cousin, the liar, and people like himself, someone he was getting to know. He walked away and in the midmorning heat boosted himself up a telephone pole. He climbed up and saw for himself what his father saw—miles and miles of trees and houses, and a future lost in the layers of yellowish haze.

37579534 ()
c2